AND WHERE HAVE YOU BEEN?

DO YOU KNOW HOW LONG I'VE JUST BEEN TWIDDLING MY THUMBS, WAITING FOR YOU TO TURN UP?

IT'S LIKE YOU THINK THIS IS ALL ABOUT YOU OR SOMETHING.

funny
kid

HarperCollins *Children's Books*

funn

written and illustrated by <s>Matt Stanton</s>

poop head

First published in Australia in 2018 by HarperCollins *Children's Books*
A division of HarperCollins Australia Pty Ltd
Published simultaneously in Great Britain by
HarperCollins *Children's Books* in 2018
HarperCollins *Children's Books* is a division of HarperCollins*Publishers* Ltd,
HarperCollins Publishers
1 London Bridge Street
London SE1 9GF

The HarperCollins website address is:
www.harpercollins.co.uk
1

ISBN 978–0–00–822024–2

Internal design by Matt Stanton
Typeset in Adobe Garamond by Kelli Lonergan
Author photograph by Jennifer Blau
Printed and bound in England by CPI Group (UK) Ltd

MIX
Paper from
responsible sources
FSC C007454

To my good buddies,
Max and Louella.

I hope this makes you laugh!

Come on.
Humour me.

I know, I know.
You thought that was my job.

This is the super-weirdest way to start a book ever.

Here's what we're going to do. If you're a girl – yes, you, hello! – please just skip to page 15.

Oh, don't look at me like that. I just need to say some things privately to the boys that'll probably make you mad, so I'm being ... thoughtful!

As I said, it's a very weird way to start a book, but don't worry. You're not being left out. After this, there's a section just for girls that the boys aren't allowed to read either.

I can trust you to do this, can't I? You're not going to tell me that you'll skip the next bit but then actually read it? Because if you read it, you'll probably be mad at me, and then if you're mad at me, I'm going to know you read it. Then I'll be mad at you because you promised you wouldn't, but you read it anyway. So we'll both be mad at each other and we won't have even started the book yet! No one wants that!

FOR BOYS ONLY!

Okay, boys. First, have a quick look around and check there aren't any girls reading this. Did you check? You're sure? Not your sister? Not your mum? Even if you have a pet cat, and that cat's a girl, then she shouldn't be reading this section either. Okay? Good.

We have to talk about something quickly, before the girls come back.

Girls are gross. Like, really gross. For a start, they smell funny, right? Like strawberry lollies or something. They'll say it's their lip balm, which in itself is disgusting. Have you ever tried that stuff? It's like getting grease out of a tube and smearing it on your lips and then never wiping it off! They just walk around with slimy lips like ABSOLUTELY NOTHING IS WRONG WITH THAT!

But it's not just the lip balm. It's the giggling. I mean, do you see us boys giggling like that? They tilt their heads towards each other as though their brains are talking, and they look over at us and giggle. It's not like we've said anything particularly funny either. We haven't done some awesome trick or told this great joke. It's just because ... well, actually, I have no idea why!

Anyway, I've gotten distracted. The reason I wanted to talk to you privately for a minute is because I have a feeling this book may turn into a … oh, I can't even say it. I'm a bit worried that this book is going to be … well … a love story.

I know! I'm SO SORRY! It's disgusting.

It's not meant to be a love story, and maybe it won't turn into one, but I have this horrible feeling … that it might. You know, like one of those movies your mum likes that she makes you watch while she says things like, 'But it's so sweet!' and 'It's just the most beautiful film.' And all you want to say is, 'I wanted the one with all the lasers … and monsters … and monsters with lasers … who explode.'

So, I just wanted to start the book by saying I'm really sorry and I hope it doesn't turn out awful or sweet or anything.

Okay, thanks, boys, and bye.

GIRLS! YOU CAN COME BACK NOW!

All right, are we all back? Good. Thank you, girls, for not reading that last section. It's your turn now.

Hey, boys. Do you mind just standing over there for a minute? Yeah, yeah, I know I'm a boy too, but I just need to talk to the girls for a second (mostly to make sure they weren't listening to our private conversation).

You had your turn, all right? Can we just be cool about this? Thanks. I'll buy you all candy.

FOR GIRLS ONLY!

Okay. Hello, my sisters!

What? Why are you looking at me like that? Is it because I made you skip the last section? Did you feel left out? I know, I know, I'm sorry …

No? That's not the reason you're mad? It's the candy! I just told all the boys I'd buy them candy and I didn't feed you anything. I am SO SORRY! I can buy you candy too. Or chocolate. Do you want chocolate instead? Don't say flowers. I don't do flowers. I hate flowers.

Still mad?

Okay, this is a fun guessing game, isn't it? NOT.

You're not mad because you felt left out and it's not because of the candy. Hang on …

You didn't … did you?

YOU READ WHAT I WROTE TO THE BOYS!

I can't believe you did that! What did I tell you? I said I needed to talk to them privately! Don't you even understand what *privately* means?

So, now I have to explain why I said what I said. Look, as you read this book, it could turn into a love story, and if it does, that will be embarrassing for me. Why? Because I'm an eleven-year-old boy with a reputation to protect. School can be a mean place sometimes, right?

I thought if I told the boys the whole 'girls are gross' thing, then it might help me out, because I have no idea what way this story will go. But I didn't mean it! I don't think girls are gross. I even love lip balm! Who wouldn't want their lips to taste like strawberry lollies? I mean, you and I both know boys are *way* grosser than girls. Boys pick their noses. Boys fart. Boys fart and pick their noses at the same time. I should know! I am one!

And we're not really annoyed about the giggling. We just feel ... left out.

You're not going to forgive me, are you?

Okay.

Well, look, I'm sorry.

This was a terrible idea.

Let's bring back the boys and get on with it.

And you can have candy too.

... Yes, and chocolate.

... And yes, sure. Sure. I can buy you movie tickets as well. And flowers ...

NO! Not flowers!

BOYS!
YOU CAN COME BACK!

Right, we're all together again, so we can get started.

Why are you boys looking at me like that? Oh, you read the girls' bit too, didn't you?

Well, this whole thing is a disaster, isn't it?

Look, the point I was trying to make is that boys think girls are gross and girls think boys are gross. I don't know why we think that. I don't know where it comes from. Maybe they taught it to us in kindergarten? I don't remember. And each year it gets a little worse. As we got older, us boys refused to invite the girls to our birthday parties and vice versa. Now that we're in middle school, we play in different parts of the playground, we eat our lunch separately and we DO NOT sit next to each other on the bus.

Who keeps making all these rules?

Boys on one side. Girls on the other.

Then, at some point, something happens. A kid from one side falls in love with a kid from the other side.

This ABSOLUTELY DOES NOT HAPPEN to me, by the way.

But it happens to some people, or so I've heard, and that's when everyone begins to lose their minds.

A boy might start to think he'd like to hang out with one of the girls. That's a hard thing to do, though, because someone decided that he is supposed to be standing over here and she's supposed to be standing over there. They don't think they can talk to anyone about it, because otherwise their friends might think they're trying to switch teams. But they're not trying to switch teams! They just want to hang out with someone on the other team for a bit!

IS THAT SUCH A BAD THING?

Anyway, my point is I don't know what happens next. But something must happen, because somehow, at some stage, boyfriends and girlfriends happen.

Which is, of course, disgusting!

As we've established, someone made these silly rules where girls are supposed to say that boys are gross and boys are supposed to say that girls are gross.

And I'm a boy, so all girls are definitely gross.

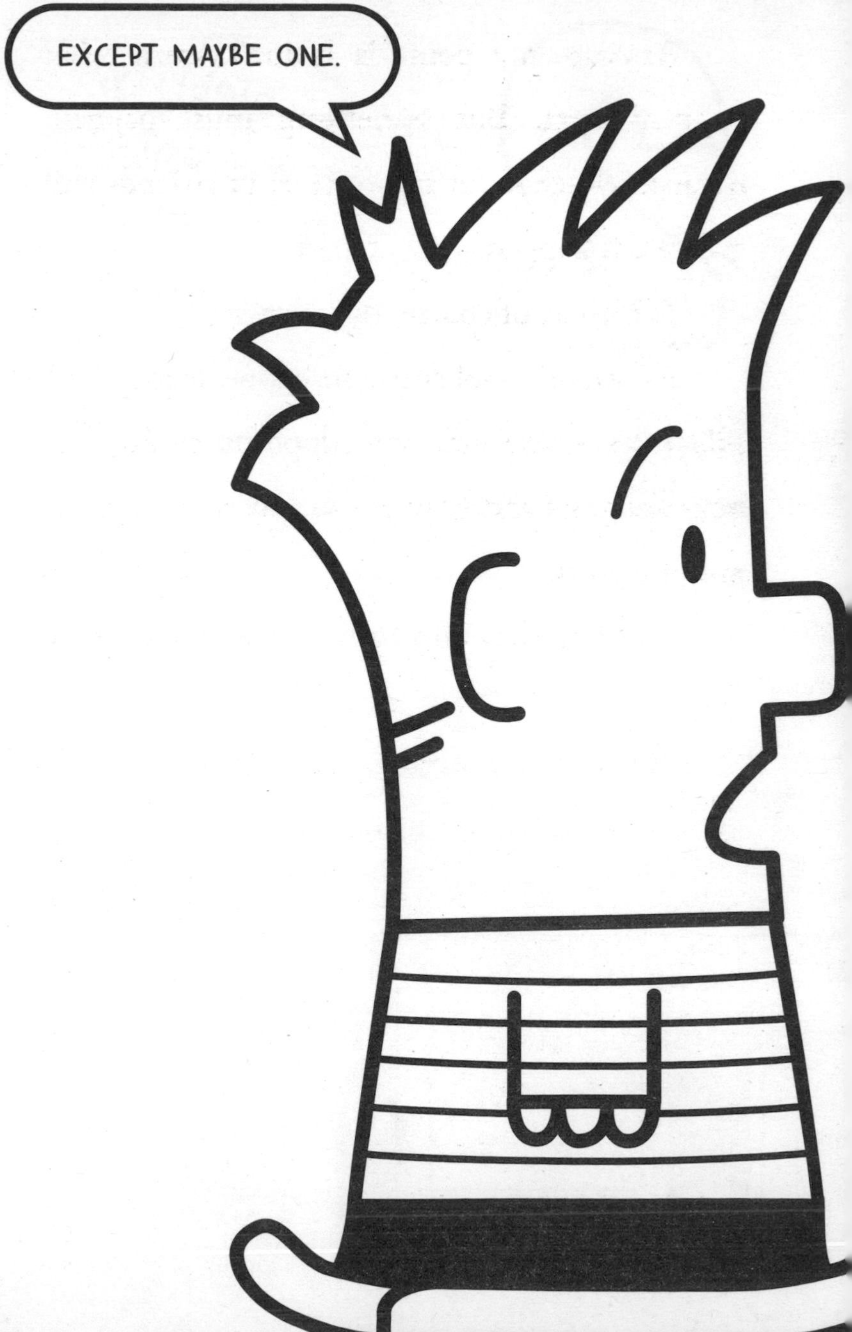
EXCEPT MAYBE ONE.

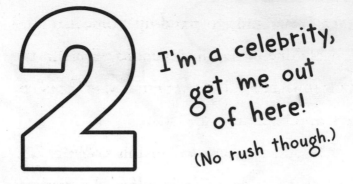

2

I'm a celebrity, get me out of here!
(No rush though.)

'Hey! Is that Max Walburt, the funny kid?'

It's Sunday morning and I'm walking down the main street of Redhill. The guy calling out from across the road is from our local fresh food market, Pick-A-Pickle.

If you're wondering why they call me the funny kid, this is all you need to know: I'm

eleven years old, a stand-up comedian and probably one of the most famous people in the whole town of Redhill after I starred in the talent quest and became a superstar.

I'm still getting used to this celebrity life. With all the autographs, the selfies, the strangers telling me they have a tattoo of my face on their bottom, it can be quite overwhelming!

I won't lie though. It's pretty fun being a celebrity. You just need to have boundaries to protect your privacy. For example, I insist on a maximum of twenty selfies per day ... per person. All right, if you insist. You can have twenty-one.

I wave back at Mr Pick-A-Pickle. I should probably know his actual name, but he's not famous, so there's not much point bothering to learn it.

I'm walking with Duck (yes, I have a pet duck) and Hugo (yes, I have a pet friend). Hugo isn't really paying attention. He's busy scribbling in a notebook.

Oh, did I forget to mention? Hugo is writing my biography. All famous people write their life story (or, like me, get someone else to write it for them). You might think I'm too young to publish my life story, but you're wrong. I'm eleven!

'What have you got so far?' I ask.

'Um ... I'm not sure if I should read it to you as we go along, Max. If it's going to be a true, hard-hitting account, then I can't have you looking over my shoulder. What if I need to write something you don't like? Know what I mean?'

'Why would you need to write something I don't like? What's not to like?'

'I don't know, Max. Maybe you do something embarrassing, but it's an important part of your journey as the funny kid and so it should be in the book?'

Hugo doesn't seem to understand how this works. I'm beginning to wonder if he's the best person to write my life story. I look down at my feathered friend. Maybe Duck should do it?

Of course that's a ridiculous idea. Duck is *way* too busy.

I turn back to Hugo. 'All you need to do is write down the amazing adventures I have in my life.'

'It's not that easy, Max,' Hugo replies, shaking his head.

'Sure it is. Take right now, for example. You can write: One beautiful Sunday morning, Max and Duck stroll down the main street of Redhill.'

'What about me?' Hugo asks.

'What about you?'

'I'm here too!'

'Oh, sure, but you're the author, so you have to be invisible. You can't be a character in the book too, otherwise it'll be a book about you! And no one will want to read that!'

Hugo grumbles something, but I continue.

'So, one beautiful Sunday morning, Max and Duck stroll down the main street of Redhill, and everywhere people call out of shop windows, "Hey! Funny kid!" As he walks by the pet store, all the fish in the window stop swimming and say, "I wish I was that kid's fish. He's really famous." Even the mayor of Redhill calls out, "Hey, Max! You're the funniest kid I've ever met!"'

'Yeah, but it totally could've.'

Hugo looks very confused. 'Where are we walking to anyway?'

'We're going to Pip's house.'

'Who's Pip?'

'The new girl,' I reply.

Pip has just moved to Redhill and she'll be coming on our school camping trip tomorrow. I don't like her or anything, because she's a girl, but I just thought I'd ask her if she wanted to hang out with the funny kid for a bit.

'We're going to see if she wants to come to the park with us,' I say.

'Why would she want to do that?' Hugo asks.

I don't think Hugo quite understands just how famous I am.

3

I'm not nervous. I'm not nervous. I'm not nervous.

Okay, so it turns out Pip must be a rich kid. Mum told me she thought the new family was pretty well-off, but this house is massive!

I count the levels of windows ... two, three ... five? I can't even tell. There's a small balcony jutting out above the front door held up by pillars. Pillars! A pathway goes up from the footpath to the front steps and on each step is a sculpture of a different animal. A lion, an eagle, a ...

'What sort of animal is that last one?' Hugo asks.

'I think it's a ... a pear,' I answer. 'The body of a bear and the head of a pig.'

'A pear? I've never heard of that before.'

'Most people haven't,' I reply. 'Okay, Hugo, Duck, you wait here.'

Duck quacks and raises an eyebrow at me as if to clear his throat and beg my pardon.

'What? You guys can just hang here … behind this tree … where no one can see you. Pip and I will come and meet you in a second!'

Hugo and Duck sulk. I don't have time for this sort of negativity.

As I walk up the path towards the grand front steps, I realise I have no idea what I'm going to say. I suddenly start to feel a little nervous. That's weird. I'm super famous. Famous people aren't supposed to get nervous. I'm not quite sure what's going on, but either I'm nervous or there's a war between worms and butterflies happening behind my belly button.

I pass the lion, the eagle and the … pear and look up at the door. There's a giant knocker in the centre that I have no hope of reaching. When God was making me, he did an awesome job on my face, but got lazy by the time he got down to my legs. There's not much to them.

On second thoughts, maybe I'll give this a miss today. I'll just see Pip tomorrow on the way to camp.

I'm about to walk back to Hugo and Duck when I notice a curtain move in one of the windows. Oh, no. What if Pip's already seen me? It would be pretty strange if she then watched me walk away back down the path.

I'm stuck. Okay, well, here goes.

I jump and try to reach the knocker, which of course I can't, thanks to my sausage-dog legs. I hope Pip wasn't watching that. Why don't people have kid-friendly knockers anyway?

Bang-bang-bang. I just knock straight on the door.

I turn and check on Hugo and Duck. I wave my hand to try to get them to hide behind the tree. Hugo just waves back. Ugh.

Suddenly the door opens.

'Hi, Pip, I –'

But it's not Pip. It's a man in a dressing gown.

WHO ARE YOU?

'I'm, um, Max,' I say. 'I think … maybe I have the wrong house?'

'You're not looking for me?' the man asks. I can't take my eyes off his very shiny, boofy black hair. That can't be real, can it?

'Um, no. I was looking for …'

'That's so disappointing.' The man frowns.

'What is?'

'That you're not looking for me. We've just moved in and I heard the door knock and I got really excited thinking you were my first visitor.'

'Well, I mean, I am sort of,' I say.

The man screws up his nose a little. He's not buying it.

'Do you play chess, Max?'

'Um. No. Not really.'

'Because I *love* chess. Unfortunately I never have anyone to play it with, because my

family hates it. Well, that's not entirely fair –
Pip sometimes humours me.'

My ears prick up at that. 'Pip?'

'Yes, Pip. My daughter,' the man replies.

'Ah …' I say. It's all making a bit more sense.

'You're a friend of Pip's?' he asks.

'Well … not really.'

YOU'RE *NOT* A FRIEND OF PIP'S?

'Well, yes, I mean, no, um …'

Pip's dad holds out his hand to save me the trouble of trying to work out my words and suddenly calls into the house, 'Pip! Max your not-friend is here to see you!' Then he turns back to me. 'I still don't understand why you wouldn't want to be friends with Pip?'

'She doesn't like you?' he asks.

'No, ah, well, I don't know.' This is going terribly!

'I can't understand why she wouldn't like you. I mean, you're so good with words.' Pip's dad grins. 'I'll go get her.'

He turns and walks back into the house. That's when I realise two things:

1. I haven't been breathing.
2. My armpits have gone soggy all of a sudden.

4

Have you ever noticed that the word 'hospitality' has the word 'hospital' in it? Weird.

I look up from my soggy armpits and see Pip standing in the doorway. She's holding a cardboard box in front of her. It seems to have notebooks and a pencil case and different-coloured markers sitting inside it.

MAX? HELLOOOO?

Jeepers! I haven't said anything yet. I raise my eyes again and open my mouth. 'Aa-ugh.'

What was that? Why did those words not come out right? That was supposed to be, 'Hey there, Pip – how are you doing?' Quick. Try that again!

'Ugh-ah-cough!'

Oh, man! I just coughed right in front of her! I get my hand up over my mouth in time, but that means my soggy armpit is showing. Aarrgghhh!

What's going on? My mouth is completely dry. I can't even talk. How did that happen?

Pip chuckles. 'Are you okay there, Max?'

I nod and then manage: 'You don't have a glass of water, do you?'

Cough! Splutter! Cough!

Pip nods slowly. She looks like she's trying to work out why this kid from her new school has just turned up on her doorstep, behaved like a bumbling idiot in front of her dad and then coughed all over her while showing off his sweat-soaked armpits. Oh, and he's desperately pleading for water. Nothing weird about that!

I'LL POP TO THE KITCHEN AND GET YOU A DRINK.

She disappears back inside.

Okay, Max, I think. You have a moment to pull yourself together and give yourself a pep talk.

'Come on, Max!' I whisper. 'You're the funny

kid! You're famous all over Redhill! What's gotten into you? Talking is your thing! You were born to talk. When Pip comes back, you're on. Let those words flow, buddy. Even better, choose something you're going to say *before* she comes back so that you're all ready. Look at this box she's left behind. Ask her about what's in it. Excellent. All right. You're ready. Let's do this.'

'Do what?'

It's Pip. She's back with the glass of water and heard me talking to myself. I can't possibly think of a good way to answer that, so I do what any normal person would do and completely ignore her question. Instead I take the water.

'Thank you,' I say and drink. Pip doesn't say anything. I don't say anything. And suddenly I realise … we're having an Awkward Silence!

And then – you're never going to believe this – Pip says, 'Are we having an … Awkward Silence?'

THE
AWKWARD SILENCE

THE THING ABOUT AWKWARD
SILENCES IS THEY BECOME EVEN MORE
STRESSFUL WHEN YOU REALISE YOU'RE
HAVING ONE, BECAUSE EVERY SECOND
YOU SPEND DESPERATELY TRYING
TO WORK OUT WHAT TO SAY,
THE WORSE IT GETS!

PLUS, WHILE YOU'RE
SPENDING ALL THIS
TIME THINKING
ABOUT THE
AWKWARD SILENCE,
STILL
NO ONE
IS
TALKING.

Arghhh! Pip named it. She said the words 'Awkward Silence'! That makes it SO much worse. Now I can't convince myself that she hasn't noticed! This is terrible.

'Ah … no, I don't think so.' Sometimes denial is the only option.

Pip smiles. 'I think we were. It went for a really long time.'

'It was a while, but I was just about to say …'

'Oh, sorry if I interrupted!' Pip's grin gets bigger.

'Um. I was just wondering … well … I was just heading to the park and I thought I'd see if you … wanted to come … too.'

'Oh, that's so sweet, Max. Thank you.'

I almost give myself a high five, but that would be really strange. I think I've probably used up all my strange points today already.

'Unfortunately I need to keep unpacking,' Pip says, pointing down at the box. 'I have lots to do before we go camping tomorrow.'

'Oh … yeah, sure. No problem.' I'm really glad I didn't do the high five.

'Who's that boy near the tree?' Pip asks, looking over my shoulder.

'That's just Hugo. He follows me around mostly.' I don't want to talk about Hugo right now! He's supposed to be hiding behind the tree!

Pip looks at my empty glass. 'Would you like some more water before you go?'

Before you go. Bummer. I was just getting warmed up.

'Yes, please,' I say, thinking it will at least give me a reason to hang around a bit longer. I hand her the glass and no sooner has she taken it from my hand than …

5 What was THAT?

It hits me like a cold, wet rhinoceros falling on top of me from a great height. Or maybe just from the second-floor balcony. It takes me half a second to realise I have not been squashed by a soppy rhino, but rather that I am completely soaking wet and standing in a giant puddle.

'TYSON!' Pip yells.

I stare at her. She looks furious. She also looks like she's trying not to laugh.

I don't understand.

I think I'm in shock.

What just happened?

Why am I drenched?

I look up at the balcony above and that's when I lock eyes with the kid who must be Tyson. He's laughing hysterically and holding an empty bucket in his hand. I decide, without even getting a good look at him yet, that his face looks like a butt. You would have to have a butt-face to pour water over a complete stranger!

He manages to say that in between fits of laughter. He's got one of those annoying hiccupy laughs too. I don't know who this punk is, but I know already that I never want to see or hear him again.

Pip has her hand over her mouth, but when I look more closely, it's like her eyes are laughing all by themselves. She sees me looking at her and starts shaking her head as if she's trying to make herself stop laughing! *How could she?*

'I'm … so … so sorry,' she whispers.

I look down at my clothes, my shoes, my hands. It's like I've just climbed out of the washing machine! And I'm freezing!

But I don't feel cold for long. Something starts to warm me up, from my tummy to my ears. Pure, red-hot rage!

I look back up at Tyson, who is still shaking with laughter as he climbs over the railing, grabs on to a nearby tree branch and swings across before sliding straight down the tree, hopping over the garden and suddenly standing right next to me. Yep, his face does look like a butt.

Oh, I'm going to have trouble working out which end to kick when I send him to Jupiter and back.

'What?' I splutter. My fists are clenched tight. I'm about to explode.

'My twin brother,' Pip repeats. 'He didn't mean it. Did you, Tyson? You didn't mean it.'

She must be able to see the lasers that are about to shoot out of my eyes and make her brat-brother disintegrate.

'Of course I meant it!' Tyson laughs. 'You don't pour water on someone by accident!'

'Tyson!' Pip exclaims.

He looks at me, chuckling. 'You did ask for more water.' Then. He. Shrugs.

I'm about to grab Tyson by the ears, swing him upside down over my shoulder and throw him in the recycling bin (even when you're mad, it's important to recycle) when I suddenly realise I have a problem.

As much as I have never disliked anyone more than I dislike Tyson right now, he is Pip's brother. If I do to Tyson what I want to do to Tyson, Pip probably won't talk to me. I may want to pulverise Tyson, but I want to be able to talk to Pip more.

One look at Tyson's grinning face and it's obvious he knows this. Oh, this little thug is smarter than he looks. It seems I'm going to have to give this some more thought.

I turn to Pip. 'I'll see you tomorrow for camp,' I say.

'See you tomorrow, Max!' sings Tyson.

'You're coming to camp as well?'

'Of course I am, buddy!'

'Bring it on,' I grunt.

As I walk away, I hear Pip ask her brother, 'Why do you always have to prank people?'

'You're just mad because you suck at pranks. That was a good one,' he replies.

'I do not suck at pranks!' Pip says.

'Of course you do. You're a girl,' Tyson says, laughing.

I leave them to their sibling fight and slosh down the path, all the way back to Hugo and Duck.

I'm delighted to see Hugo wiping tears of laughter from his eyes.

'So I take it she's not coming to the park with us?' he asks.

Tread very carefully, Hugo. I might still put someone in the recycling bin before this day is over.

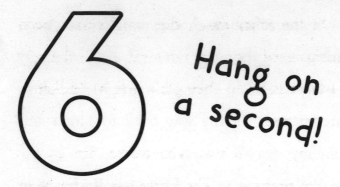

6 Hang on a second!

I would like to pause the story for just a moment, because I'm not sure you're quite appreciating how mature I am.

Most kids, if they'd just had someone pour water all over them, would have done something extreme – you know, like put the person in a shopping trolley and push them down a very large hill.

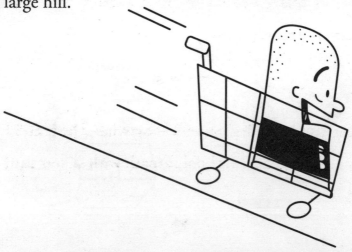

On the other hand, they might have been so embarrassed they just ran away … all the way to the airport, where they got a one-way ticket to Antarctica.

In my case, it was even worse. See, in my town, I'm pretty much as famous as Spider-Man at this point. And when you insult someone who's actually a really big deal, there should be consequences. At least some jail time.

So I had every right in that moment to do something a little undignified to the twin-from-hell. But I didn't and the reason is not just because I was flipping freezing cold!

I didn't because I am a mature and wise eleven-year-old.

* * * *

The sun hasn't been up for long when Duck and I meet Hugo in the school carpark with all our stuff for camp. We have backpacks, pillows, sleeping bags and a tent that we're going to share. Plus, we have a few extra emergency supplies, like my entire collection of Captain Kickbutt comics and many, many cans of beans. Hugo likes to pack beans when he goes to things. Poor kid can get very hungry.

We walk over to the Redhill Middle School bus. Apparently this rust bucket is going to take us camping.

YOU KNOW WHAT I CAN'T UNDERSTAND?
THEY DON'T LOOK THE SAME.

Some of the other kids have already arrived. Pip and Tyson don't seem to be here yet.

'They look sort of similar,' I say.

'Max, twins aren't supposed to look similar. They're supposed to look *the same*.'

'But Pip's a girl and Tyson's a boy, Hugo,' I reply. 'They couldn't look *exactly* the same.'

PRECISELY.
WHICH IS WHY I'M NOT SURE I BUY
THIS WHOLE 'TWINS' THING.

'Not all twins look the same. Only *identical* twins.'

'Looking the same is what *makes them twins*,' Hugo says, shaking his head. 'That's why I always keep an eye out whenever I'm anywhere new in case I see someone who looks exactly like me and I realise I'm a twin! You never know!'

Sometimes I feel sorry for Hugo. Life's going to be tough for him.

'Good morning, idiots!'

I don't need to turn around to know who that is. Have you heard of Yin and Yang? Don't worry, it's not another set of twins. It just means that for every good thing, there's an opposite bad thing. There's even a symbol for it that looks like this:

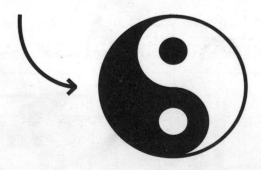

Basically, for every light, there's a shadow. For every hero, there's a villain. For every ray of sunshine, there's a puddle.

For every Max Walburt, there's an Abby Purcell.

'Morning, Abby,' I say.

'How did you manage to get the water out of your ears, Max?' she asks. *Oh, no! How did Abby hear about Tyson's prank?* It's like Abby can hear my thoughts, because she explains, 'Pip called me last night. Did you forget we're friends, Maxy boy?'

To be honest, I had forgotten. I have trouble understanding how someone as cool as Pip could be friends with my mortal enemy.

'It sounds like Tyson got you so good!' Abby says.

'There's no need to feel sorry for me,' I reply. 'I'm fine.'

'Playing pranks is harder than you think, Abby.'

'Yes, I can see that,' she replies with a thick layer of sarcasm. 'A real intellectual challenge.'

'What's even harder, though, is being the bigger kid,' I continue. 'Of course the first thing you want to do is get back at the person who pranked you, but it takes someone pretty special to rise above the silliness and not get revenge. I'm kind of like that Gandhi* guy. You should tell Pip that.'

'You're way too short to be the bigger kid, Max,' Abby says.

'Watch me.'

---

*I can't actually remember who Gandhi is. I think he did good stuff though, like help people be peaceful or something. Either that or he's the weatherman on Channel 11.

7

Operation: Smuggle Duck!

Once everyone has arrived with their stuff, Miss Sweet explains that we have a long bus trip ahead of us. She says we should put our tents and pillows and sleeping bags in a pile so Mr Bert, the bus driver, can store them in the compartment underneath the bus.

'Miss Sweet, I have a question,' Abby pipes up next to me. 'I'm thinking about safety, and I'm sure you and Mr Bert will do a great job looking after us, but I think it would be good to bring my dog Steve along on this trip. He's a police dog, so he'll be able to help protect us. Is that okay with you?'

Oh, no! I can't stand that giant, disgusting dog.

'He's not a police dog, Abby,' I say. 'Just because your mum is a police officer doesn't mean that horrible mutt is a police dog. He's just your dog.'

'Abby, you can't bring your dog on our camping trip, I'm sorry,' Miss Sweet says as she starts looking down a list to check everyone is here.

'But who will keep us safe?' Pip asks. My ears prick up at that. This is my chance.

I, UH, I CAN DO THAT, PIP.

I make my voice a little lower so I sound more manly.

Abby bursts out laughing.

'Are you girls worried about something in particular?' Miss Sweet is choosing to ignore me, it seems. 'Why don't you think you're going to be safe?'

GUNKER DRAGONS.

What?

Miss Sweet looks confused, as though she's trying to work out what's going on.

'Gunker *what*?' Mr Bert asks.

Abby and Pip glance at each other, their eyebrows shooting upward.

GUNKER DRAGONS. DON'T YOU KNOW ABOUT GUNKER DRAGONS, MISS SWEET? MR BERT?

I'VE NEVER HEARD OF THEM.

If the girls looked nervous before, they look slightly terrified now.

'I don't think I want to go on this trip, Miss Sweet,' Pip says.

'Yeah, I have a headache,' Abby says.

'Is it a migraine?' Pip asks.

'I think it's a migraine,' Abby confirms. 'Miss Sweet, I need to go home.'

Miss Sweet squats down in front of them. 'Girls, what's going on here? Who told you about Gunker Dragons?'

'Google,' they say together.

Miss Sweet begins to explain that you can't believe everything you see on the internet (which is stupid, because of course you can – that's where I learnt about the cockroaches that race each other by riding miniature Russian hippopotamuses). I find myself getting quite excited about doing some Gunker Dragon research myself, once we get back from camping. I'm not normally interested in learning stuff, but in this case, Abby and Pip seem genuinely scared, and that could prove quite useful for me.

Maybe I should offer to stay up at night and keep watch. I mean, I would probably fall asleep, but that's all right. Pip wouldn't need to know that. All I'd have to do is stay up a little longer than her.

'Excuse me, Miss Sweet?' Pip interrupts the teacher's little speech. 'Why is there a duck standing there?'

I turn quickly and sure enough, Duck is standing right behind me. I really need to teach him to get a bit better at not being seen.

'He's mine,' I say.

'You have your own duck?' Pip asks.

I decide to play it cool. 'Sure! Doesn't everybody?'

She laughs. 'Is *he* coming on camp with us?'

'Of course –'

'Not,' Miss Sweet interrupts. 'Come on, Max. If I've just said Abby can't bring her dog, I'm not about to let you bring your duck on the bus.'

'But what if Duck can help keep Abby safe by fighting the Gunker Dragons for her?' I ask with a grin.

Abby scowls at me.

'Ducks are my favourite!' Pip says.

The hair on my arms stands up. *Did she really just say that?*

I turn to Duck and he winks at me as if to say, 'Oh. Yes. She. Did.'

This is amazing! Ducks are her favourite animal and I have my own duck! That settles it. Duck *has* to come camping with us.

I turn to Miss Sweet. 'At least let me say goodbye?'

'Quickly,' she replies and faces the rest of the class. 'Everyone else, line up for Mr Bert, please.'

I take Duck over behind the bus.

Duck points his beak at my T-shirt.

'You want to hide inside my T-shirt?'

Duck nods.

'It's going to make me look pretty fat,' I say.

Duck looks cranky.

'I'm not saying *you're* fat. I'm saying that if I hide you in my T-shirt, it's going to look like I suddenly got a very big tummy. Miss Sweet might have some questions.'

Duck seems satisfied with that.

'What if I hide you under the bus with the tents and stuff?' I suggest.

'Don't worry. It's safe under there.'

Duck scowls at me and crosses his wings. I didn't even know ducks could do that!

He nods to my backpack.

'You want to hide in my backpack?'

Duck shrugs as if to say, 'It's not ideal, but it's better than your last insane suggestion.'

I unzip my backpack and we both look inside to see if there's room.

'I guess I don't really need to take *all* those undies.'

Foolproof bus strategy.

I join the line for the bus. My backpack wriggles. Poor Duck. I've left a crack in the side zipper so he can breathe. Pip was quite impressed by Duck. I'm beginning to think that Duck might be my secret weapon.

I want to show Pip I've hidden Duck in my backpack and the best way to do that will be to sit next to her on the bus.

But who-sits-next-to-who is a complicated business. It's time for a plan.

The first question is who should get on first. An inexperienced bus-sitter would tell you that the best strategy is to let Pip get on first.

Then I can simply sit next to her. Right?

WRONG!

If I just sit down next to Pip, then that's going to draw a lot of unwanted attention (if you've forgotten why, please go back and re-read Chapter 1). The way to get around that issue is to wait until there aren't too many seats left, so it's just like I happened to sit in the empty seat next to Pip, because there weren't too many options. However, there is way too much risk in that scenario. For a start, Abby and Pip are friends, so Abby will probably sit next to her. If Abby doesn't, Tyson might sit next to Pip, or some other random kid. This is not the time to leave things to chance.

Instead the correct strategy is actually for me to get on first. This is a scenario I can control, because I can make sure no one sits next to me. Then if Pip gets on towards the end of the line, I will have one of the few seats left.

So I push my way through to the front of the line.

'Hey!'

'Max!'

'Don't push in!'

'Did you just quack? I swear someone just quacked.'

The door opens and I climb onto the bus, taking a seat about halfway down. I look out the window. Pip is towards the back of the line. Perfect.

'Hey, Max, what are we going to call your book?' I look up and see Hugo taking his backpack off to sit down next to me.

I put my backpack on the seat next to me.
It quacks uncomfortably.

'Why not?' Hugo asks, confused.

'Ah …' Quick. I need a reason. 'Because you
have to … sit behind me. If you sit behind me,
then we can both have a window seat. Then I
can turn around and we can work on my book
while we look out the window. You know, for
inspiration.'

'O-kay,' Hugo says slowly, like he thinks I've
lost my mind. He takes the seat behind me.

The bus starts to fill up, and I keep my bag on the seat and avoid looking anyone in the eye.

Finally Abby, Pip and Tyson get on. When Abby reaches me, she looks at my backpack sitting on the seat and raises one eyebrow. It doesn't matter how many times she does that, it still gives me the creeps!

CAN YOU MOVE YOUR BAG, MAX?

Oh, no. I don't want Abby to sit next to me! That's not how this is supposed to go. That's the worst-case scenario!

'Why don't you sit next to Hugo?' I ask.

'Why don't *you* sit next to Hugo?' Abby says. 'He's your friend.'

'No,' Hugo butts in, because he knows the answer to this one. 'I have to sit behind Max so we can work on his book while we're looking out the window for inspiration.'

'Idiots,' Abby mumbles and sits across the aisle from Hugo, next to Layla.

Phew! That was close. Pip's next. Here we go. My plan has worked perfectly.

I move my backpack onto the floor at my feet. It quacks again. Pip smiles.

CAN I SIT NEXT TO YOU?

'Oh … sure, if you want,' I reply. Only she wasn't talking to me.

'Sure you can!' Hugo says.

WHAT?

Pip sits down next to Hugo.

And Tyson sits down next to me.

Aaaarrrrgggghhhh!

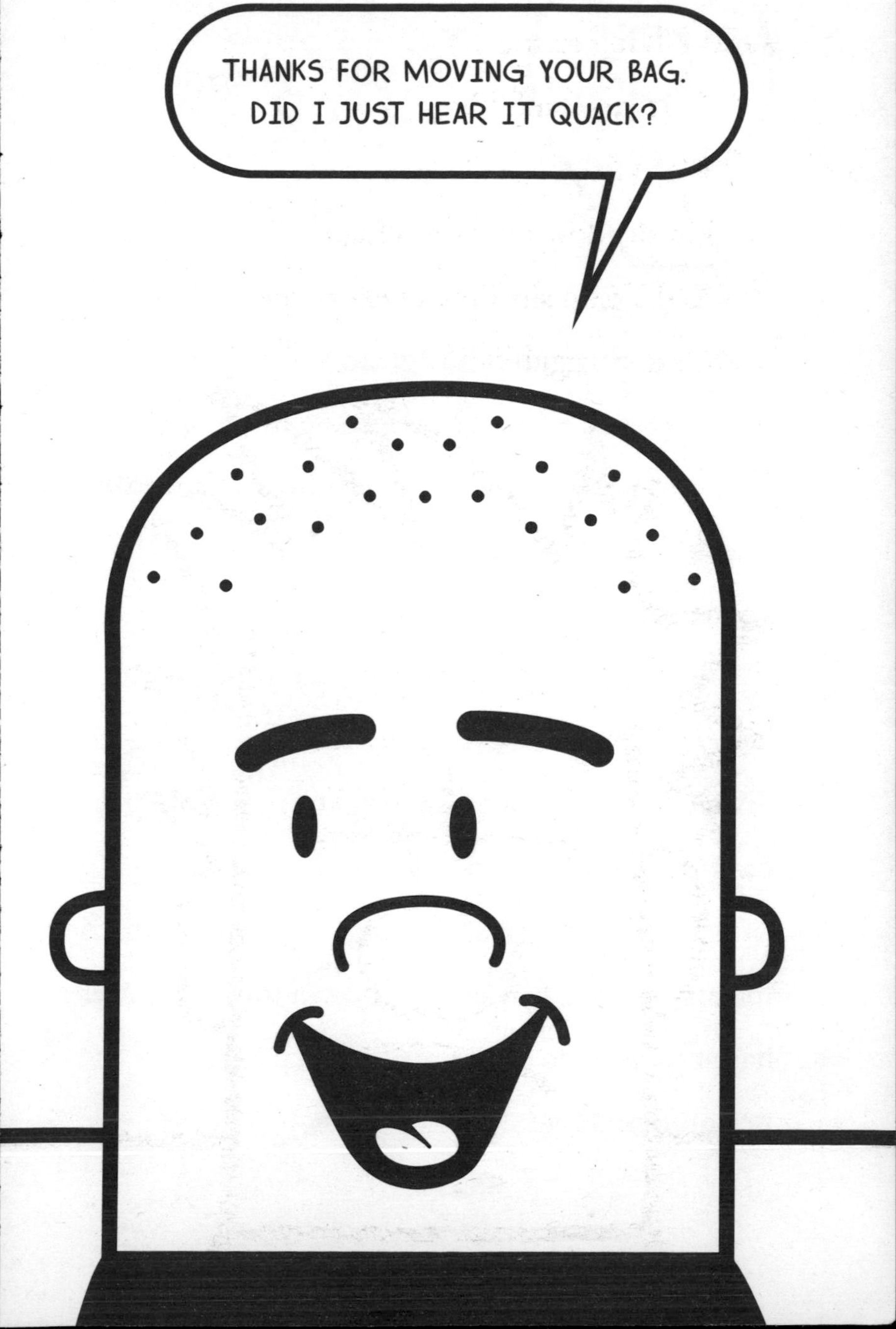
THANKS FOR MOVING YOUR BAG.
DID I JUST HEAR IT QUACK?

Tyson's giving me travel sickness.

Well, isn't this great. Just great.

I'm stuck with the last person in the universe I want to be sitting next to. (And yes, that means I would have preferred Abby Purcell, so that's saying something!)

I'm drinking from my water bottle, not because I'm thirsty but because I'm trying to distract myself from just how terrible this plan has turned out.

Tyson has spread his legs out wide, which means I'm squashed against the window. Whatever happens, you do not want to touch legs with the person next to you!

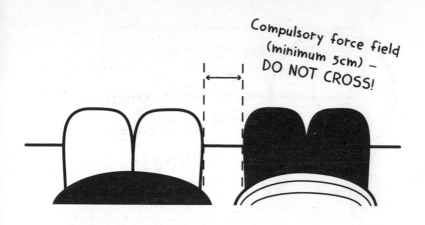

Everyone knows you need to keep a nice little air barrier between your thigh and the thigh next to you, but to achieve that you have to work together. I don't know what things were like at Tyson's old school, but he doesn't seem to understand this whole teamwork thing very well.

I keep drinking.

'You thirsty there, buddy?' Tyson asks. 'You really do like water, don't you?'

'Shut up,' I grunt.

Hugo taps me on the shoulder. I ignore him. He keeps tapping. Then he leans his head between Tyson and me.

'What book?' Tyson asks.

'I'm writing a book,' Hugo replies.

'Are you really? That's amazing,' Pip says. 'What's it about?'

'It's about Max.'

Abby leans across the aisle. 'You're really writing a book about Max? But why? His life is so boring. You'd be better off writing a book about Pip and Tyson – their life is much more interesting.'

'What do you mean?' Hugo asks.

'Pip and Tyson are adopted, and their new dad is like a really famous actor, and so now they're super rich and can have anything they want.'

'He's not that famous,' Pip says.

'Yes, he is,' Tyson says. 'He's going to be in a Christmas movie with Justin Bieber.'

I keep drinking my water and pretend not to be listening. We've left Redhill behind now and are travelling along the highway under a big blue sky.

'Max is really famous too!' Hugo says. 'Max, are we going to work on your biography now?'

'Maybe we can help?' Pip asks.

That gets me turning around in my seat, accidentally kicking my backpack as I do. *Quack.*

'What keeps quacking?' Kevin calls out from the front of the bus. That kid has really good hearing.

As I shuffle around onto my knees, I realise I better stop drinking. I'm starting to need to pee and it's not like there's a toilet on this bus.

'I didn't realise you were famous, Max,' Pip says.

'Oh, I'm not *that* famous,' I say, waving my hand like a really famous person would.

'He's really not,' Abby adds.

'People call him the funny kid,' Hugo says.

'I like to make people laugh.' I shrug.

'I like laughing,' Pip says. 'Is the book going to be funny, Hugo?'

'Hilarious,' Hugo replies.

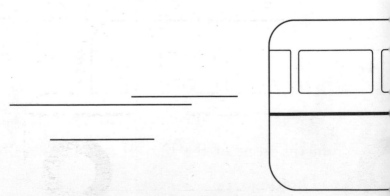

Ooh. I really do need to go to the bathroom. I squirm a bit to try to un-squash my bladder. Maybe if I can give it a little more room, it won't feel like it needs to push all that pee out. Be patient, bladder. Now is not a good time. (What? You don't talk to *your* bladder?)

Tyson gives me a funny look.

'I just need to come up with a title,' Hugo says. 'Do you have any ideas?'

'Me?' Pip says. 'Oh, I don't know. Um …'

'What about *Living with a Big Head: The Life of Max Walburt*?' Abby suggests.

Everyone laughs at that. I glare at Abby. Polite laughs are cheap laughs. That wasn't even funny.

Hugo continues. 'I was trying to think of something to do with jumping puddles or using a metaphor to do with water, after what happened yesterday. I feel like that's a good symbol for what the book could be about.'

'How about *Wet Walburt and Other Soggy Jokes*?' Abby says.

Again everyone laughs. I'm trying to think of a good comeback, because heaven knows we could all do with an *actual* joke right about now, but to be honest, I'm incredibly distracted by my bladder. It wasn't so bad until I turned around. I squirm a bit more, and Tyson looks at me and chuckles.

'How about *Needing to Pee: Adventures of the Funny Kid*?' he suggests.

Oh, no! I thought I was hiding it really well.

'I don't get it,' Hugo says.

Tyson turns to me. 'You need to pee, don't you, Max?'

'What? No! Of course not.'

Abby grins. 'Are you sure?' she asks. 'You look a little uncomfortable there.'

'You were drinking quite a lot of water before,' Pip chimes in.

'I'm fine!' I say. 'Thank you, everyone, for your concern.'

Then we go over a bump on the road.

Aarrgghhh! I think a bit of pee just came out! I look down at my pants in horror and everyone watches me do it.

'You do need to pee!' Tyson says.

'I said I'm *fine*!' I turn back around and sit properly, kicking the backpack again. *Quack.*

'Seriously! Who keeps quacking?' Kevin asks. Those ears. Amazing.

I just need to focus. That's all I need to do. Focus on not peeing, ignore what everyone says and just stay focused.

'Drip.'

What was that?

DRIP.

It's Tyson, softly making a dripping water sound right next to me. 'Drip.'

I can hear giggling. Then I hear Abby whispering, 'Ssssshhhhhh,' like a tap running with water. More giggling.

SSSSSHHHHHH.

SPLASH. SPLASH.

Pip has caught on and is adding her sounds. All these water noises are making it very ... hard to ... hold ... on. I can't believe they're doing this! And Hugo too!

TINKLE. TINKLE.

The kids around us are laughing.

'Stop it! Just stop it!' I yell.

'What's going on back there?' Miss Sweet calls out and everyone stops.

I take a deep breath. Thanks, Miss Sweet, my bladder is about to explo–

'Row, row, row your boat, gently down the stream,' Tyson starts singing.

AAAAARRRRRGGGGGHHHHHHH!

The whole bus is laughing now.

Pip leans forward. 'You really are *very* funny, Max.' Then she sits back and joins everyone in singing the tune.

10 A toilet meeting.

We stop at a petrol station on the way to our campsite, and I'm so busting I run across the carpark and into the toilet cubicle without even taking off my backpack. The feeling of finally being able to piddle when you've been about to pop has to be one of the best feelings in the whole world.

Quack.

Now that the wee is out, it's like my brain is free to start working again and I remember – oh, that's right – Duck's still inside my backpack.

I reach down and undo the zip so Duck can stretch his wings.

He seems a little cranky with me as he flaps out of the backpack and onto the toilet floor. (Ew, in bare feet too.) Duck may believe I am his mummy, but that doesn't stop him being annoyed at me for keeping him zipped inside a backpack for the last hour. He does a little shake.

Someone knocks on the door. 'Come on, Max! Other people need to go too.'

Oh, really? Maybe I should just sit here and sing 'Row, Row, Row Your Boat' from the comfort of this incredibly relaxing toilet seat.

'What am I going to do, Duck?' I ask my little feathered friend. 'This Tyson kid is becoming a problem.'

Duck nods and then realises there's a piece of old toilet paper stuck to his foot.

'He seems to be pretty good at pranks and for some reason, he's decided I'm the one he wants to be pranking. Famous people aren't supposed to get pranked!'

Duck is only half listening to me. He's trying to scrape the toilet paper off his foot.

'Careful, Duck. Who knows what that toilet paper was used for before it was dropped on the floor?'

Duck looks up at me and tilts his head to the side as if to say, 'We're in a toilet, dingle-splat. What do you think it was used for?'

'Hey, Max! Come on! We're waiting!' someone calls from outside.

I'll take my sweet time, thank you very much. That'll teach you all to try to make me pee on the bus.

'I thought the best way to impress Pip was to just ignore Tyson, but I think I was wrong.

The only way to stop Tyson ruining my reputation is to prank him back,' I tell Duck as I flush the toilet.

'Oh, finally!' someone outside exclaims.

I wash my hands and turn to Duck.

WE'RE GOING TO HAVE TO GO TO WAR, DUCK. PRANK WAR.

I nod at the backpack. 'You need to get back in.'

Duck puts his wings on his hips.

'Come on, Duck. You have to. If Miss Sweet sees you, she'll leave you on the side of the road.'

Duck blows a raspberry and his little shoulders sink. He knows I'm right. Then he reaches down and pulls the toilet paper off his foot with his beak! Ew, gross! It's a public toilet, dude!

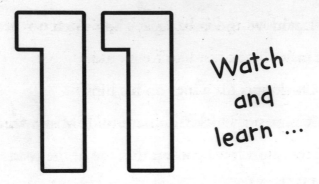

11

Watch and learn …

I open the toilet door with the confidence of an action hero heading into battle. Kevin pushes straight by me, leaving his backpack on the ground outside.

There are two bathrooms and all the kids in our class are lined up, waiting to go. I watch Tyson laughing with Pip and Abby, and I wait for my time.

'Are you ready for this, Duck?' I whisper over my shoulder. 'We're going to have to move very fast.'

After a while, Kevin comes out and Tyson

goes in, throwing his backpack against the wall of the toilet block just like Kevin did.

'Go-go-go!' I whisper … to myself.

I run past the other kids and slide across the gravel to Tyson's backpack.

I unzip it and quickly start pulling out all his stuff and putting it on the ground.

'What are you doing?' Hugo asks.

'You'll see!' I say, removing a lunch box, a drink bottle, a jumper, a stuffed rabbit.

'Why are you taking all the things out of Tyson's backpack?' Ryan asks.

'It's okay,' I reply with a grin. 'I'm about to put it all back in.'

I take the now-empty backpack and shake it upside down. A couple of candy wrappers and a banana peel fall out.

'Max?' It's Pip. 'What are you doing to my brother's backpack?'

'Oh, just a harmless little joke. Don't worry. He'll love it,' I say.

Actually, I don't think he will love it. But hopefully everyone else will.

Now that the backpack is completely empty,

I put my hand in and pull the whole backpack inside out. It takes half a minute to fold in the straps and make sure the edges are right, but in the end it still looks like a backpack, only now all the stitching is on the outside and the straps are on the inside.

Most importantly, so is the zipper.

I hear the toilet flush. Quick! He better wash his hands, because I still need about thirty seconds.

I take all of Tyson's things and shove them into the inside-out backpack. Pip realises what I've done and starts to giggle. The others laugh too.

'I told you I'd put everything back,' I say.

Now for the final step. I reach my hand inside the backpack and find the little zipper tag. It's simple to grab while the backpack is open. I pull it across, doing up the zipper from the inside.

HOW TO DO THE
BACKPACK PRANK

1. EMPTY EVERYTHING
OUT OF THE BACKPACK.

2. FLIP THE BACKPACK
INSIDE OUT
(LIKE A T-SHIRT).

3. PUT EVERYTHING
BACK INTO THE
BACKPACK, NOW THAT
IT'S INSIDE OUT.

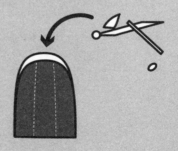

4. REACH INSIDE THE
BACKPACK AND CAREFULLY
CLOSE THE ZIPPER.

PRANKED!

Closing the backpack is easy. What is almost impossible is opening it again when the zipper is on the inside.

I finish just as the toilet door opens. I leap up, throwing the bag exactly where Tyson had left it and blending back into the crowd of kids. There's lots of giggling as everyone waits to see what will happen.

Tyson steps out of the toilet and seems somewhat surprised to find most of his class standing there, looking at him with big grins on their faces.

WHY ARE YOU ALL LOOKING AT ME?

The cool thing to do here, I realise, is to slip away as though I don't even need to see his reaction. That's what a famous kid would do. I look towards the bus and see Mr Bert filling the tank with petrol. Miss Sweet is standing with Abby in front of a big map of the national park near the road.

I head on over, but on the way, I hear a very clear, 'What's up with my backpack? Who did this? How am I supposed to get it open?' followed by massive laughing.

I grin to myself and whisper to Duck:

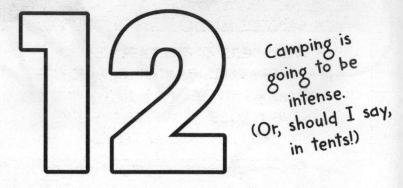

12

Camping is going to be intense. (Or, should I say, in tents!)

Miss Sweet wants everyone to look at the big map before getting back on the bus. We might all be standing around, but most people are much more interested in watching Tyson try to open his backpack.

'Stupid thing!' he's muttering.

'Tyson, shh,' Miss Sweet says. 'Everyone, this is the map of the national park where we will be camping for the next two nights.'

'How … on earth did you … even …' Tyson grunts. The class giggles.

Miss Sweet ignores him and points to a big star on the map.

WE'RE HERE AT THE ENTRANCE TO
LAKE QUIET NATIONAL PARK. IN A MINUTE,
WE'RE GOING TO GET BACK IN THE BUS AND
DRIVE ACROSS TO WHERE WE'LL BE
SETTING UP OUR TENTS.

I look over at Tyson. He's squeezed his fingers inside his backpack, through the little hole where the zip finishes, but to open it up, he's got to grab the tiny zip tag inside the bag and push it away from himself. If you've ever tried to push a zipper instead of pulling it, you'll know it's almost impossible.

He notices me and I try to raise my eyebrows as if to say, 'That'll teach you to mess with the funny kid,' but instead I accidentally wink at him. He looks very confused. Stupid eyebrows.

'Abby, you look worried,' Miss Sweet says.

'I'm fine,' Abby replies.

'Are you thinking about the dragons again?' Pip asks. Abby nods. Pip turns back to the rest of us. 'Last night Abby was showing me on the internet that the most recent sightings of Gunker Dragons have been in Lake Quiet National Park.'

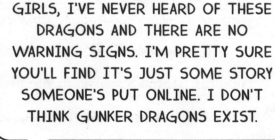

GIRLS, I'VE NEVER HEARD OF THESE DRAGONS AND THERE ARE NO WARNING SIGNS. I'M PRETTY SURE YOU'LL FIND IT'S JUST SOME STORY SOMEONE'S PUT ONLINE. I DON'T THINK GUNKER DRAGONS EXIST.

'People do say they're supposed to be extinct …' Abby says softly.

'There you go, see? They all died a long time ago.' Miss Sweet smiles reassuringly.

'… but then there have been sightings recently. No one knows for sure,' Abby finishes.

Pip pulls a phone out of her pocket and holds it up. 'I brought this so I can take photos if we see a dragon. You know, for proof!'

Miss Sweet shakes her head. 'Pip, you can't bring a phone on camp. It's against school rules.'

'I'm sorry, Miss Sweet. I didn't know,' Pip says. 'It doesn't make calls. It's just for taking photos and videos. My dad gave it to me because he knows how much I love nature and he likes it when I take photos. He says I have "an eye", whatever that means. I was just thinking that Lake Quiet is going to be so beautiful, so I want to be able to capture it. Can I keep it? Please?'

Miss Sweet sighs and then nods. 'Okay, kids, back on the bus!'

I turn to Abby and Pip. 'Don't worry, girls. Everyone knows dragons aren't real.'

Abby glares at me. 'Do you ever read history books, Max?'

'Ugh. Why would I do that?'

'What about horror stories? Do you like those?' she asks.

'Totally! Horror stories are awesome,' I reply. I have no idea where she's going with this.

'Well, sometimes history books have horror stories in them, Max. Only they're much scarier … because they're true.' And with that, she gets back on the bus.

She is a very strange girl, that Abby Purcell.

* * * *

We travel into Lake Quiet National Park for another half an hour or so. The trees get really tall and the road gets really bendy, but eventually we arrive at a clearing next to a huge lake.

We all get out and there's almost no sound at all. No cars driving by. No dogs barking. No next-door neighbour yelling at the garbage truck for running over his bin again.

'I think I know why they call it Lake Quiet,' Hugo whispers.

'You're a very clever kid, Hugo. Have I ever told you that?' I reply.

'Never,' Hugo says. 'You have *never* told me that.'

It's time to set up our tents.

Setting up a tent feels a bit like trying to build a house with chopsticks and three garbage bags. Hugo and I start by unwrapping our garbage bags and then sticking all the chopsticks together. Unfortunately that means we just end up with one really long chopstick.

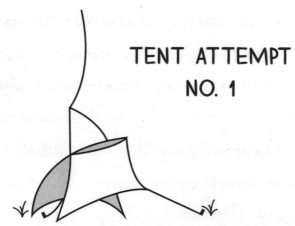

TENT ATTEMPT NO. 1

We begin again and this time we end up with five shorter chopsticks, which makes an awesome scarecrow but not a very good shelter.

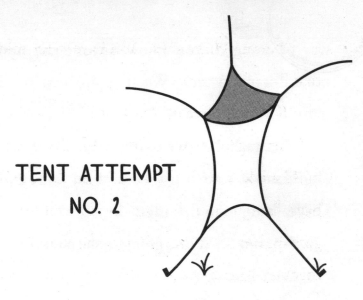

TENT ATTEMPT
NO. 2

'How are you getting on there, boys?'

I look up and see Abby and Pip standing there, smirking at us. Behind them, their tent is set up perfectly. Ours looks like a weird sort of plastic salad.

'We're fine,' I say.

'It looks like you're having a bit of trouble,' Pip says.

'It's much harder than –'

I cut off Hugo. 'No trouble at all. We were just seeing if there might be a more ... creative way of doing it. You know, anyone can have a normal-looking tent. We thought we'd try and make ours two storeys.'

'Oh, really? A two-storey tent?' Abby scoffs.

'Exactly. Like bunk beds!' I say with a grin. I'm really digging this idea!

Pip smiles. 'Who's going to sleep on the top?'

'Me!' I reply.

'I'm not sure I'd be so keen to volunteer for that,' Abby says.

'Why?'

'Well,' Pip says, 'whoever is on top is going to fall the furthest when the monsters get you in the middle of the night.'

'Or even if it just gets windy,' Abby adds. 'Is that what you want, Max?'

'Hmm. Good point. Hugo, you can have the top bunk!' I say.

'Thanks, Max.'

'Then again,' Abby continues, 'whoever is on the bottom level is probably going to have the person on top fall and squash them in the middle of the night.'

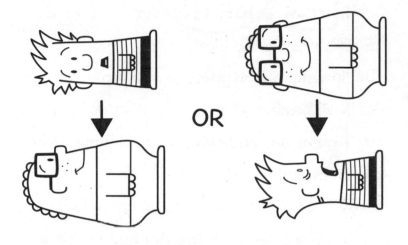

I look at Hugo. Ah … um … 'Let's just set it up normally, eh?'

Hugo nods.

Pip and Abby wander off, which means I can quietly ask Miss Sweet to come and set up our tent for us.

13 Scary stories!

The afternoon goes pretty quickly, and before long, we're all sitting around a campfire that Mr Bert made and Miss Sweet is telling us it's almost time for bed. All we've done since we arrived here is set up tents, tables and chairs, move logs for the campfire and then sit on the logs and have dinner.

'What sort of holiday is this?' I complained. Miss Sweet then took ten minutes to explain to us that we weren't on holiday. We were spending two nights out by the lake to learn to appreciate nature. Apparently nature needs us to appreciate it more or something. It's so needy.

Dinner was some sort of slop, although that might be overselling it. A greeny-creamy-blueyorangey sort of colour, it was like soup, except lumpy, and I think I saw it wriggle.

I sneak away from the food area to a spot behind our tent where I've made a home for Duck. He seems quite happy to polish off my dinner for me, which is helpful, but it also means I'm going to bed hungry. I decide to take some of the bread I hid for Duck into my tent to eat later. After all, I've got to eat. I'm a growing boy!

When I come back, Pip wants to tell scary stories.

We roast marshmallows in the fire and Mr Bert tells us about a haunted house with the ghost of a walking, talking pig called Bronwyn.

Layla tells a story about a baby that was bitten by a radioactive goat (crazy kid!), and Ryan tells one about a politician who turns into a maniac at night and steals everyone's money (in other words, he stays exactly the same).

'Abby, do you have a scary story?' Pip asks.

Everyone looks at Abby. She actually seems quite nervous. She shakes her head, then nods, then shakes, then nods.

'Come on, tell us about your scary dragons,' I say, because this makes me look tough and brave.

'But that story is true,' she replies. 'So it actually is scary.'

'I bet it isn't.' I glance over at Pip.

'It is!' Abby says. 'And it's even worse than that because it's about this place. That's why I got so nervous when I realised we were coming to Lake Quiet. I've read stuff about this place.'

'Like what?' Hugo asks.

Abby just shakes her head.

'Oh, come on!' I say. 'How scary can it be?'

Abby scowls at me. 'Okay, fine. Lake Quiet, where we are right now, is where the Gunker Dragons used to live.'

'What do you mean when you say "dragons"? What were they actually like?' Kevin asks.

'Like ones that breathe fire?' Hugo asks.

I blow a raspberry. 'Of course not, Hugo. Someone's tricked Abby with all this nonsense.'

'I've seen photos, idiot. When we get home, you can look it up.' Abby turns to Hugo. 'Of course not fire-breathing dragons. Gunker Dragons are like Komodo Dragons, these giant lizard things. They used to inhabit this whole region centuries ago, but they became extinct.'

GUNKER DRAGON

'So more like dinosaurs?' Ryan asks.

'Exactly,' Abby replies. 'They lived in the water like giant crocodiles and then came out at night to hunt their prey while it slept.'

Hugo shudders and looks over at the lake.

'Big deal!' I say. 'I'm not scared. You even said it yourself, Abby. They're extinct!'

'Well, technically yes.'

'Technically?' Tyson asks.

'There have been sightings,' Abby says. 'About once a year, a camper or hiker reports that they think they've seen one dragon that still lives here. Or they'll report things going missing from their campsite in the middle of the night.'

'And on that note, time for bed!' Miss Sweet announces. 'Don't worry, Abby. There are no monsters out here.'

'Not monsters. Gunker Dragons,' Kevin murmurs. 'Thanks for freaking us out, Abby.'

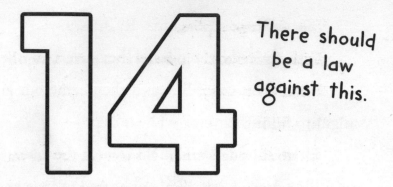

14

There should
be a law
against this.

When I climb into our tent, Hugo is already there in his pink ballerina-flamingo pyjamas. There's not much room to move in here.

I demand Hugo closes his eyes while I get into my own PJs. I'm about to pull on my pants when I smell it.

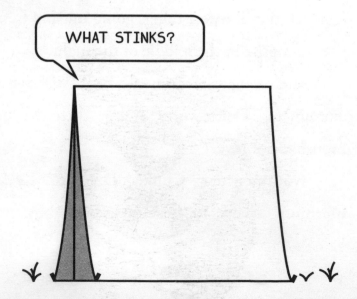

WHAT STINKS?

'Sorry,' Hugo replies.

'Did you seriously just fart in a tent, Hugo?'

'I said I was sorry.'

'In a TENT!'

'It's these beans that I brought for extra snacks.' He points to a whole bag of tinned beans next to his sleeping bag. 'Sometimes they do funny things to my tummy.'

It's so disgusting. It smells like how a skunk would smell if it had come home from its job at the sewage works, after eating an egg covered in parmesan cheese and forgetting to brush its teeth.

I desperately want to flee the tent, except I'm not wearing any pants. So instead I'm stuck, half naked and marinating in Hugo's stench, inside our little garbage-bag house.

'There's something I've always wondered,' Hugo says, still sitting there, farting with his eyes closed. 'In order for you to smell something, does some of it have to actually go into your nose?'

'What do you mean?'

'Are you smelling my fart because a bit of fart air came out of my butt and floated through the tent and then got sucked into your nostril?'

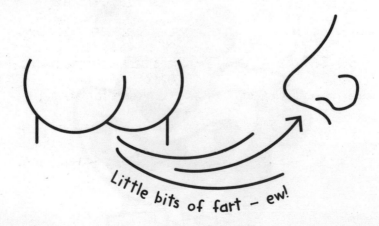

Little bits of fart – ew!

I gag and yank on my pants. 'Hugo, shut up!'

'It's a pretty gross idea, don't you think? That maybe a bit of my butt air is now inside *your* body.' He pauses as I leap into my sleeping bag. 'Can I open my eyes yet?'

I decide not to answer that and just change the subject. 'How's my book going anyway?'

'Well, I've been thinking about that,' Hugo says as I try to get comfortable. 'I've decided I'm not going to discuss it with you any more. You've been squashing my artistic vision.'

'What are you talking about?' I ask as I push one leg down into my sleeping bag. 'It's my book.'

'See, this is the problem,' Hugo says, his eyes still closed. 'I'm actually quite enjoying writing, but if I'm the writer, then that makes it *my* book. Not yours. You can write your own if you want, but you're the subject of *my* book, so I'm just going to watch you and write down what I see.

Maybe I'll let you read it at the end. I haven't decided yet.'

'You're not making any sense.' My sleeping bag is twisted. I try to stretch it out. 'This book is supposed to be about how awesome I am. I can help with that! Besides, I'm not giving you permission to write about me without letting me read it.'

FREEDOM OF SPEECH, MAX. I DON'T NEED YOUR PERMISSION. I CAN WRITE IT ANYWAY AND I CAN MAKE IT ABOUT WHATEVER I WANT.

I push my other leg down into the sleeping bag. Hang on a minute. What is that?

I just touched something with my toe. Something cold and squishy. Something kind of long. I poke it. It just keeps going, all around the bottom of my sleeping bag. I have a bad feeling about this.

HUGO?

'Yes.'

'There's something in the bottom of my sleeping bag.'

'Something like what?'

'It's long and windy and cool and a little bit ... scaly,' I explain, listening to the words as I say them. Why would there be ...?

'Oh, that's a snake for sure,' Hugo says.

AAAAAARRRRRRRGGGGGGHHHHHHH!

I scramble desperately to get away from the reptile at my feet, but it's actually surprisingly difficult to remove oneself from a sleeping bag quickly! My feet get tangled, the sleeping bag slips and slides, and I can feel the snake moving as I move. It's around my knees! I'm kicking and thrashing like I'm trying to run a race lying down.

'Are you okay?'

'Get me out of here!' I yell, finally freeing my legs. I jump up onto my feet, leaping away from the sleeping bag and crashing into the side of the tent. 'Where's the torch? Give me the torch!'

I snatch it out of Hugo's hand because he's not nearly fast enough. I point it straight at my bed, enough to see a toy rubber snake half hanging out of my sleeping bag.

And that's when I hear Tyson laughing hysterically from the tent next door.

I am going to pull that stupid kid's ears off!

He's not the only one laughing either. There is giggling coming from all across the campsite!

OH, THIS PRANK WAR IS ON!

Then I turn to Hugo. 'It's okay. It's not a real snake. It's just Tyson getting revenge for what I did to his backpack.'

'Phew.' Hugo breathes a sigh of relief. 'Hey, can I open my eyes yet?'

15

Wakey, wakey!

When the sun hits our tent the next morning, I'm already awake. Super-soldiers in prank wars never sleep.

I'm lying in my sleeping bag, listening to the birds.

So many lovely tweeting birds. I've never been so happy to listen to them. Whistles and squawks, cheeps and twitters. A big smile spreads over my face.

'What's that noise?' Hugo mutters, still half asleep.

'That's the beautiful sound of a choir of feathered angels,' I reply.

Hugo opens his eyes and looks at me as though I just farted. Buddy, I'm not the one in this tent with a gas problem. I can tell he's listening to the birds now too.

'They're quite loud,' he says.

I grin. 'Very loud.'

'What's going on?' Hugo asks, looking suspicious.

SHOULD WE HAVE A LOOK?

We unzip the tent, poking our heads outside. There are no birds on the ground. No birds in the trees. Hugo looks confused.

'Check out the tent next door,' I whisper.

We swivel our heads towards Tyson's tent and Hugo's eyes open wide. I've never seen so many birds at the one time in my entire life. They are completely covering the tent – flapping, squawking, fighting. You can hardly even see the tent – it's just a giant hurricane of feathers.

'What the –?' Tyson suddenly calls out.

Hugo looks at me.

'I got up in the middle of the night and covered Tyson's tent in breadcrumbs,' I say. 'It's important for the birds to be able to have some breakfast. It's the most important meal of the day after all.'

Tyson must feel like he's being attacked by Big Bird in there.

We watch as everyone else comes rushing out of their tents to see what's going on. They all look over and slowly start to laugh.

Tyson is still screaming like he's just sat on a hedgehog and it's actually scaring the birds away. We all watch as the zip on his tent comes down and Tyson falls out onto the grass. Of course, crashing out of his tent scares the rest of the birds away, so when he finally glances around to see what was causing the cyclone he woke up to, there's nothing there.

'You all right there, Tyson, buddy?' I ask.

He looks over at me, incredibly confused.

'Revenge is sweet,' I say quietly to Hugo.

'You're pretty good at this prank war thing,' he says. 'Can I help?'

'Sure,' I say. 'You should probably clean up those leftover bits of bread.'

Not sure that's quite what Hugo had in mind, but then it doesn't really matter. Duck has come out of his hiding spot and is helping himself to breadcrumbs for breakfast.

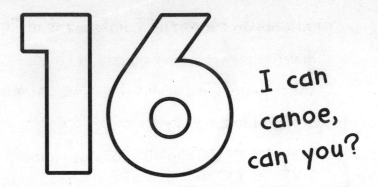

16

I can canoe, can you?

Breakfast was chaos because it turned out Mr Bert does not know how to make eggs, one of the camping toilets was broken and a couple of kids seemed to be missing some of their stuff. Layla's basketball was gone (don't ask me why she brought that), Kevin lost his hairbrush (I know why he brought that – his hair is superb!) and Miss Sweet almost lost her patience.

She managed to just hold on to it though, and after breakfast, she dragged us all down to the edge of the lake to a row of orange canoes. We're all in our life jackets getting instructions about paddling to the other side of the lake for a picnic lunch. Hugo and I stand next to Pip and Abby.

'Did you see the prank I pulled on your brother this morning?' I whisper to Pip.

'Don't you think crocodiles are monsters?' Pip says, smiling, and before I can answer, she adds, 'I can't wait to go canocing.'

'Who has been in one of these before?' Miss Sweet asks.

I have, of course, *never* been in a canoe, but now is hardly the time to tell the truth. I look at Pip and raise my hand along with a couple of other kids. I'm pretty sure Pip is impressed.

'Excellent,' Miss Sweet replies. 'Those who have done this before can take the picnic baskets.'

'When have you been in a canoe, Max?' Abby asks as she and Pip line up their canoe next to ours. I can tell she doesn't believe me.

'Oh, too many times to count. I was pretty much born in a canoe. It's so easy. You'll see,' I say as I put our picnic basket, Pip and Abby's basket and my backpack into the canoe.

'Why are you bringing your bag?' Hugo asks.

I turn to him quickly and put my finger over my lips. Duck is in my backpack, but no one knows that. I'm going to show Pip once we're out in the middle of the lake.

'You sure you're not going to sink with all that stuff?' Abby asks.

'No sweat!' I call out, flashing my best action-hero smile and flexing my muscles so Pip can appreciate my toned biceps. Pip's not looking. Abby screws up her face and pretends to vomit. The girls jump into their boat and glide straight out onto the water.

We push the canoe out a bit. Hugo goes to climb in. It takes him a moment to work out which body part should go in first. He starts with one leg, but he can't lift it high enough. Next, he tries to reverse in, bottom first, but the whole canoe starts to tip.

'Woah,' I warn him, trying to hold the boat steady. He looks at me, shrugs and just dives in headfirst.

He's in the canoe, which is a good start, he's just upside down. The canoe shakes wildly as Hugo flips himself over.

My turn and, just like Hugo, I can't quite swing my leg over. So I attempt a graceful spring-jump in, holding the front of the canoe. My legs come off the ground, but I can't get my tummy over the side. Try again.

Only, when I go to put my feet back down on the sand by the lake, I realise we've started to drift away from the edge and I can no longer reach solid ground. We're now floating out into the lake with Hugo in the back and me hanging on to the outside of the front of the canoe.

'Max! Why are you down there?' Hugo asks.

I try to swing my legs up, but just succeed in splashing myself in the face. Ugh.

'I'm stuck, Hugo. Pass me your paddle, would you?'

Hugo shoves his paddle towards me, but manages to whack me in the stomach in the process, pushing me straight off the canoe and – *SPLASH!* – into the water.

I say hi to a couple of fish while I'm underwater and then swim around the side of the canoe. Hugo reaches down and gives me a hand, making it a little easier for me to clamber in.

'You're right, Max,' Abby calls out from the middle of the lake. 'It's *so* easy! Just don't you dare drop our lunch overboard!'

Grrrrrrrr …

COME ON, HUGO. WE HAVE TO CATCH THEM!

'Why?'

'Just paddle like me. Quick!'

We begin paddling and turn around in a complete circle. Awesome start. I switch my paddle to the other side and try again. We just turn in a complete circle the other way. It's a great way to see the scenery, but it's not helping us get where we need to go!

'Hugo! Stop copying me! You have to paddle on one side of the canoe and I paddle on the other! Hurry!'

'I still don't understand why we need to catch them,' Hugo says as we finally move in a straight line.

'I have something … I want to show … Pip,' I manage in between puffs. This canoeing thing is hard work!

Eventually we find a rhythm and reach the middle of Lake Quiet. It's quite a large lake and as we look back at the shore, we see that there are actually a whole bunch of camping sites that are exactly like ours dotted all along the lake's edge. It makes me think that if you accidentally ended up in the wrong camp, you could think that everyone had packed up and gone home! I'll store that in my little memory-bag of pranks …

I roll my eyes. 'We are carrying all the stuff!'

'I was wondering why you brought your backpack as well?' Pip asks.

I grin at her and reach down to unzip the top of my bag. Out pops Duck's head.

QUACK.

'You brought your duck!' Pip beams.

'Where did he come from?' Hugo asks.

'Did you seriously bring your duck on camp in a backpack?' Abby demands.

Quack. Duck hops out into the canoe.

'You know how some super-famous people carry their dogs around in handbags?' I wink. 'Well, I keep Duck in my backpack.'

'That's so cool,' Pip says.

'You're such an idiot,' Abby says.

'Abby, we're on a lake,' I remind her. 'Ducks love lakes.'

'Hey, did you know there are sandwiches in here?'

We turn back and see Hugo has opened our picnic basket and found lunch. He holds up a sandwich.

WOULD ANYONE LIKE ONE?

Quack!

Before we can answer, Duck flaps his wings and charges at Hugo. Apparently when you've been squashed inside a backpack all morning, you get a tad peckish.

'Aaaarrrrgggghhhh!' Hugo screams and falls back in the canoe. 'Get it off! Get it off!'

'Help him, Max!' Pip calls out. 'Poor Hugo! The duck's attacking him!'

I leap to my feet, just like I imagine my favourite hero, Captain Kickbutt, would do.

'It's okay, Hugo! I'll save you!' I yell. 'He's going for the sandwich, not for you! Give him the sandwich!'

NO! IT'S MY SANDWICH!

'I'm coming, Hugo! Just let go of the stupid sandwich!' I try to walk, which is hard inside a very wobbly canoc.

'Never!'

Two picnic baskets and my backpack are between me and Hugo and Duck. How am I supposed to –?

'Save him, Max!' Pip shouts. I glance over at her. She's right. It's time to be a hero.

'Watch out for the –'

Abby calls.

I leap
through the
air, over the top
of the baskets, and
crash into the back of
the canoe, tipping the thing
onto its side and sending us all
headfirst into the water as the canoe
completely capsizes.

'– lunch,' Abby finishes.

17

You are not going to believe this.

'Every time I see you, you're soaking wet,' Tyson says as he sits down on the log next to Hugo and me with his lunch.

We've all made it to the picnic spot on the other side of the lake and everyone is sitting down to eat their sandwiches. Hugo and I are still dripping and feeling sorry for ourselves. Pip and Abby are sitting opposite us, scowling. Apparently they wanted lunch too.

'Mmmmm. Delicious.' Tyson finishes his sandwich and rubs his tummy with a big grin on his face. 'What a wonderful lunch!'

'Shut up,' I mumble.

Suddenly Tyson's tummy lets out an enormous rumble. We all stare and Tyson's smiling face twists into a look of pained confusion.

'You all right there, Tyson?' Pip asks.

'Yep,' he replies. *Grumble-burp-thud-ergh*. 'I need to see Miss Sweet.'

He gets up and runs to find the teacher. I wonder what's gotten into him.

Hugo leans towards me and whispers, 'I put some of my beans in his breakfast this morning.'

My eyes opcn wide and I look at my friend with a big, beaming smile. 'You what?'

WHEN MR BERT WAS HANDING OUT EGGS THIS MORNING, I PUT A WHOLE LOT OF MY BEANS ONTO TYSON'S PLATE. ONCE I GAVE IT TO HIM, HE THOUGHT EVERYONE HAD THEM. I WANTED TO HELP YOU OUT IN YOUR LITTLE PRANK WAR.

He nudges my side with his elbow and winks.

'Hugo. You. Are. Awesome,' I whisper back. 'There's nothing little about this prank war. This is going to be the nuclear strike.'

'My tummy's pretty used to them, but Tyson's going to be in all sorts of trouble,' Hugo says, proud of himself.

We look over and sure enough, Tyson is hopping from one foot to the other, pleading with Miss Sweet. I glance around us. We're in the park on the opposite side of the lake from the campground. There's no toilet over here!

'Max? Can you come here a minute?'

I realise Miss Sweet and Tyson are looking towards us.

'I didn't do anything!' I yell back. This time it's actually the truth. It doesn't seem to matter to Miss Sweet. She glares at me, so I get up and head over.

'Max,' Miss Sweet whispers when I get there. 'I need your help. Tyson's got a bit of a … situation. I need you to … help him out.'

What on earth does that mean?

She reaches into her canoe and pulls out a small shovel. 'I need you to go with your friend Tyson here into the woods over there, where it's nice and private, and dig him a quick … hole.'

'Ew! No! I can't do that!'

'Yes, you can, Max. And you will. Tyson can't really do it himself right now. Look at him.'

I look at Tyson. He's bouncing up and down and slowly starting to resemble a puffer fish in a microwave.

'Okay, quick. Go now!' Miss Sweet orders.

I glance back at Hugo, terrified. He is suddenly no longer awesome.

'*Come on, Max!*' Tyson says.

He is already hopping off towards the tree line. Oh, this is horrible. How did this even happen? One minute we're having a prank war and the next I have to dig a toilet for the enemy before he explodes!

Teachers! They ruin everything!

I drag my feet behind Tyson until I realise the longer I take, the worse it's going to be for me. I need to dig that hole and get out of there before he blows up!

I'm running now, straight past Tyson, to a spot behind some trees and then I'm digging like crazy. Quick, quick, quick!

HURRY UP, MAX!

TYSON, DON'T YOU DARE POO!

'I don't think I can hold it any longer!' he grunts.

I wave frantically at the hole. 'Is that enough? Is it deep enough? How do you know how deep to dig a toilet?'

Tyson looks down and shakes his head. 'Deeper. It's going to need to be *much* deeper.'

I keep digging like crazy. I've never done anything with this much urgency. I would rather be anywhere else in the world right now. Anywhere!

There's dirt flying up in every direction now. I'm like a dog trying to find a bone. I don't care where the dirt goes, I just want to get this hole finished and get out of here!

'I can't hold any more, Max!' Tyson yells. 'It's coming out!'

Aaaaaarrrrrrrrgggggghhhhhhhh!

I throw the shovel over my shoulder, clamber across the mound of dirt and dive for cover.

* * * *

I never look back. I never check to see the damage.

I emerge from the woods a shell of my former self. Cold. Wet. Covered in dirt and vowing never to speak of what just happened.

I really need a wash.

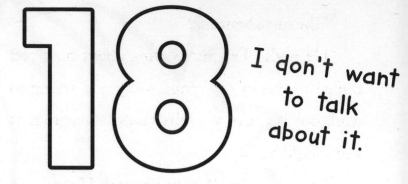

18

I don't want to talk about it.

After getting back from canoeing, there's an archery lesson with Mr Bert and an obstacle course with Miss Sweet. Then we build another campfire and eat dinner as the sun goes down.

Tyson hasn't said a word all afternoon. As traumatic as the Poop That Must Not Be Named was earlier, I think I might have won the prank war.

While we eat dinner, I can't help noticing that Hugo is staring at me and writing in his notepad.

'What are you doing?' I ask.

'I'm working on my book.'

'The one about me?'

He nods. 'I'm just writing about how you tipped us out of the canoe today and trying to work out if you're as embarrassed about that as you should be.'

I scowl at him. 'I don't like this, Hugo.'

He smiles and writes that down too.

Suddenly someone screams, and Pip and Abby come running up from the lake to where we're all sitting around the fire.

'What's wrong?' Miss Sweet asks.

'Saw what?' Ryan asks.

'A Gunker Dragon, out in the water!' Pip says.

'What did it look like?' Abby asks.

'Just like you said it would – like a big, floating log.'

'Maybe it *was* a log?' Tyson suggests. Ah, so he can speak! I was worried he might have pooed out his tongue earlier.

His sister glares at him. 'Then it dived down under the water,' she says.

Miss Sweet walks over to Pip and starts leading her towards the lake. 'Come and show me. The rest of you stay here with Mr Bert.'

The rest of us look at each other.

'Do you think it's the Gunker Dragon that took some of our stuff this morning?' Hugo asks. 'Like Layla's basketball and Kevin's hairbrush.'

'They are known to take things from campers,' Abby says.

'Oh, this is ridiculous,' I say, now that Pip's not here. 'You're making this stuff up, Abby. Or you read some stupid thing on the internet and now you think you're seeing dragons everywhere.'

Everyone giggles. Including Mr Bert. Hugo is writing furiously in his notebook once more.

'What's everyone laughing about?'

I look up and see that it's Pip who's asking! She and Miss Sweet are back from the lake.

'Nothing,' I say quickly and then desperately try to change the subject. 'Did you see the dragon again?'

'No, we didn't,' says Miss Sweet. 'We think it was just a log, don't we, Pip?'

Pip shrugs, holding her phone and not looking convinced at all. 'Maybe?'

Hugo looks up from his notebook. 'Hey, Max, maybe we should leave some of my super beans out for it. If they have the same effect on the dragon as they did on Tyson, we'll know if it's real for sure.'

I shake my head frantically at Hugo, but it's too late.

'That was you guys?' Tyson asks, his eyes opening very wide. 'You gave me the runs at lunchtime?'

'Ah …' I try to find an answer. Turns out Tyson doesn't really need one.

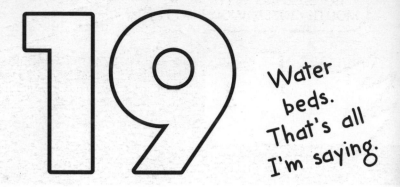

19

Water beds. That's all I'm saying.

I wake up in the middle of the night with the distinct feeling that something is wrong. In my half-asleep state, I find myself imagining Gunker Dragons, but that's not it. I feel like the ground is moving. Not like an earthquake, just gently up and down.

And it's cold. Like really cold. I shiver. Did Hugo forget to zip up the tent or something?

I think I can hear soft splashing. Hugo must be dribbling and gurgling again.

'Hugo, shhhh!' I say without opening my eyes.

'What?' I hear him reply.

There's silence then. It still feels like I'm moving though. It's so weird. I actually feel a little sick. Maybe Tyson got back at me by putting something in my dinner. No, that doesn't make sense, because he didn't find out about the beans until just before bed.

'Um, Max?' Hugo says.

'Shhhh. I'm trying to sleep.'

'I think you should probably open your eyes.' My friend sounds concerned.

'Why?'

'Just open them, Max,' Hugo says. 'Max!'

'Okay, fine!' I sit up in bed and look

All right. Okay. Stay calm. No big deal. Hugo and I are still in our sleeping bags and on our air mattresses. Our air mattresses are just floating out in the middle of the lake.

THE MIDDLE OF THE LAKE!

I quickly go to leap out of my sleeping bag, but of course that just makes the whole air mattress rock and dip wildly, and I suddenly find myself holding on for dear life.

This has to be a dream. It must be. I can't

possibly actually be in my pyjamas floating in the middle of Lake Quiet. That's the stuff nightmares are made of.

And that's when I hear the laughing.

I look back towards the shore and there, standing on the water's edge, are Tyson, Kevin, Ryan and Layla. It's not a dream. We are actually out here.

'That'll teach you to give me the runs!' Tyson calls out.

Behind them, I see Abby and Pip come running out of their tent and down towards the lake.

'What are you guys doing?' Pip yells, sounding terrified. 'Didn't I just tell you I saw a Gunker Dragon out there? It lives in the water!'

For the first time in this trip so far, I find myself genuinely considering whether these Gunker Dragons are real. I mean, of course they're not, but … what if they are?

THIS IS HOW WE'LL FIND OUT IF THE DRAGONS ARE EXTINCT OR NOT! WE'VE GIVEN THEM LIVE BAIT!

'Maaaaxxx,' Hugo is saying, very nervously.

'They're not real, Hugo, don't worry. It's just something someone made up to scare campers,' I say, but I'm not totally sure I believe myself.

'Get out of there!' Abby shouts.

'Let's just try to get back to the shore,' I say to Hugo. But I don't know how we're supposed to do that. We're out on Lake Quiet without a paddle.

I shake my head. 'Look,' I say and point towards the shore.

Hugo looks back and sees what I see. Abby has jumped into a canoe and is paddling towards us all by herself. Even though she always tries to ruin my life, and she humiliated me back at the campfire, she's still going to be the one to save us.

Which is pretty awesome, given that if there's anyone who is really convinced there's a Gunker Dragon in this lake, it's her.

'You're rescuing us?' I ask as she gets closer. We climb carefully into the canoe and head back to shore, pulling our air mattresses behind us.

'No matter how dumb I think you guys are, I don't want you to get eaten by a Gunker Dragon,' she says.

Turns out Abby Purcell is not just super annoying. She's pretty brave too.

20

Is it over?

Back on the shore, Tyson ruffles my hair as I climb out of the canoe. 'This little prank war has been fun, Maxy boy, but I'm pretty sure I win, don't you think?'

Before I can answer, Miss Sweet's voice cuts in. 'What on earth are you all doing up in the middle of the night? Max! Abby! Hugo! Did you just get out of that canoe? With your beds?' Miss Sweet is almost always calm, like unnaturally so. But it seems half the class getting up in the middle of the night and going into the lake on their air mattresses is what it takes to actually make her lose it. Well done, everyone – we finally pushed her to her limit!

'None of this is my fault, Miss Sweet. I was asleep,' I point out.

'Get back in your tents this instant! Every one of you! You kids are unbelievable!'

'But, Miss Sweet –'

'Abby! Shut it!'

We all scamper towards our tents, Hugo and I dragging our beds behind us.

Before he disappears into his tent, Tyson calls out:

DON'T WORRY, MAX!
SOMEONE HAD TO BE THE LOSER!

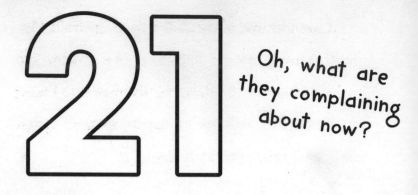

21

Oh, what are they complaining about now?

The next morning, the whole class gets a big talking-to. Miss Sweet uses her calm but very serious voice to tell us we need to be more responsible. If we're going to be able to go on excursions like this one, she has to know she can trust us. Today is our last day, so she wants us to pack up our tents now so we're not rushing to do it just before we get on the bus at two o'clock sharp. She makes us all repeat the departure time to make sure we don't miss it.

Mr Bert is nodding along, but he looks as though he probably would have been standing on the shore laughing at Hugo and me along with the rest of them if he'd been thirty years younger.

I spend most of the talk thinking about Pip. I'm beginning to worry that as cool as I think she is, she thinks I'm the loser her brother says I am.

Everyone's sent off to pack up their tents, but I don't move from my log.

Is Tyson right? Have I lost this prank war? I just can't think how I'm going to top the floating bed incident. Plus, we're going home soon.

Ugh. This sucks.

'WHO TOOK PIP'S SUITCASE?'

I look up as Abby storms around from behind her tent, yelling at the top of her lungs.

SOMEONE'S TAKEN PIP'S SUITCASE OUT OF OUR TENT AND I WANT YOU TO GIVE IT BACK RIGHT NOW!

Abby has planted herself in the middle of the clearing. Pip stands a little behind her. No one says anything.

'MAX! TYSON! Get over here right now!'

Abby's going to make a great teacher one day. Either that or she'll run a prison.

'I didn't take Pip's suitcase! Why would you think that?' I leap to my feet, keen to defend myself in front of Pip.

Abby glares at me. 'Oh, I don't know. Maybe because of the inside-out backpack, the breadcrumbs on top of Tyson's tent, the beans in his breakfast?'

Tyson comes out from his tent and joins us. 'It wasn't me. Pip's my sister. What makes you think I would –?'

'Oh, let me think,' replies Abby, the master of sarcasm. 'Maybe it was the bucket of water, the make-you-pee songs, the plastic snake in the sleeping bag or the floating beds that make you suspicious.'

'See, he's totally done more than me,' I observe.

THAT'S WHY I WON.

DID NOT.

SHUT UP! BOTH OF YOU! I DON'T REALLY CARE WHICH ONE OF YOU TOOK THE SUITCASE, BUT WHOEVER IT WAS, GIVE IT BACK RIGHT NOW!

Tyson and I both point at each other. 'It was him.'

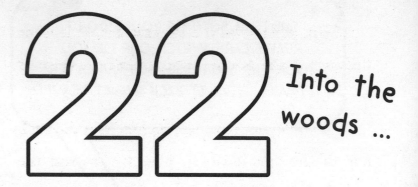

22 Into the woods ...

Abby looks like she has swallowed dynamite. So Tyson says something that's always really helpful.

'Abby, just *calm down* –'

It's like those last two words come out in slow motion. I duck for cover. She's going to rip his head off and under normal circumstances I would just let it happen, but poor Tyson has no idea who he's messing with, and it's not like I haven't been there myself once or twice.

'Where was the suitcase?' I ask quickly.

'WHAT?' Abby snaps. No one likes being interrupted when they're about to pulverise someone.

'Pip, where was the suitcase before it went missing?' I ask. Someone needs to be a voice of reason.

'It was in our tent,' she replies. 'But the back flap of the tent has been pulled open and the suitcase is gone.'

LET'S HAVE A LOOK.

We all head to the girls' tent – Abby, Tyson, Pip and me. Hugo hurries after us and even Duck pauses in packing up his little nest to inspect the situation.

Sure enough, it's exactly as Pip described. The back of their tent is open and you can see in the dirt where someone (or some*thing*) has dragged the suitcase outside.

'Look, there's a trail,' Tyson says, pointing to marks in the dirt that lead away from the tent.

Tyson follows the suitcase marks to the edge of the clearing, where the bushes start. Suddenly he gasps.

'What?' Abby asks.

We run to see what he's looking at.

There, in the middle of a muddy patch, heading into the woods, is a giant footprint.

It's not a human footprint either. It looks like a … dinosaur print.

Duck quacks.

'Do you think that's the –?' Pip asks.

'The Gunker Dragon?' Hugo gasps. 'Your suitcase has been taken by the Gunker Dragon!'

Abby steps forward slowly and inspects the footprint. 'This is just like everything I read,' she says. 'They come in at night and steal things from campers.'

'Like Layla's basketball and Kevin's hairbrush …' Pip says.

'And now your suitcase,' Abby finishes. Then she stands bolt upright and turns around. 'Does this mean it came in while we were asleep?'

Pip's eyes go wide. 'I'm pretty sure the suitcase was gone when we first woke up.'

Abby looks like she's about to cry. 'Piiiiiip, it came into the tent with us to take the suitcase!'

Hang on a minute, this is getting out of control. They really actually believe this. Time to bring some calm to this situation.

'Abby, Pip, Hugo, listen. There's no Gunker Dragon. This is clearly just one of Tyson's pranks,' I say.

'It is not!' Tyson declares. I ignore him.

THIS IS THE GUY WHO PUT HUGO AND ME OUT IN THE MIDDLE OF THE LAKE LAST NIGHT. CLEARLY HE ALSO TOOK THE SUITCASE TO PLAY ON YOUR FEARS ABOUT THE DRAGON.

'Did you?' Pip asks, turning to her brother.

'No! I think it was Max,' he says.

'Was not.'

'Was too.'

'Was not.'

'Was too.'

QUACK! Duck scowls at both of us as if to tell us to pull our heads in.

'It wasn't me either,' Hugo contributes to the conversation. 'In case anyone was wondering.'

No one was.

OKAY, WELL, NOW WE HAVE A PROBLEM. INSTEAD OF YOU BOYS SPENDING THE WHOLE TIME BLAMING EACH OTHER, WHY DON'T YOU DO SOMETHING PRODUCTIVE? SEEING AS YOU'RE SO CONVINCED THAT GUNKER DRAGONS AREN'T REAL, I THINK YOU SHOULD GO INTO THE WOODS AND FIND PIP'S SUITCASE FOR HER.

Tyson and I look at each other.

'Yeah, if you don't think they're real, then you've got nothing to be scared of, right?' Pip adds.

We look into the woods. The trees are tall in there, so the morning light can't really get in. It's dark and, well, just between you and me, a little scary. This is not where I thought this conversation was going.

Why won't Tyson just admit his prank so we can all pack up and go home?

'Um … what was in your suitcase?' Tyson asks his sister. 'Do you *really* need it back?'

Pip glares at him.

I suspect he's feeling the same way I am.

I'm *pretty* sure these Gunker Dragon things are a hoax, but that doesn't mean I'm keen to follow a potential one into the woods to find out for certain. Being out on the lake last night, it had almost felt believable that something could be lurking down in the water beneath us.

'Not so confident now, are you?' Abby says. 'Go on. If they're extinct, then there's nothing to worry about, is there?'

'Ah ...'

Quack! Duck has had enough and decides to take action himself. He marches into the woods, following the trail of the suitcase.

If Duck can do it, so can I.

'Okay, come on then,' I say and walk into the woods, followed by Tyson, Hugo, Pip and Abby. 'Let's go get the suitcase. We just have to make sure we're back before two o'clock.'

23 It can't be ...

We head into the woods in single file, following Duck. My brave little friend is short and quick, and I have trouble keeping up. Also, because I'm taller than him and the first kid in the line too, it's my head that hits all the branches on the way through.

Whack. Ugh. 'Watch out for that one!'

Every time I get walloped in the face, I hear Pip giggle, which on one hand is good, but on the other – isn't she worried about her suitcase?

It's quite easy to follow the path of the suitcase, because there are scratch marks in the dirt.

'Tyson, you really did drag this suitcase a long

way,' I say. It must be Tyson, surely. Eventually he's going to admit it.

'I told you,' Tyson replies, 'I didn't do it! Why would I take the suitcase? Pip's my sister! This looks exactly like the sort of prank *you* would pull.'

'Why would I prank Pip?' I argue back. 'I –'

Oops. In the heat of the moment, I almost said 'I like her'. That was close.

'You *what*, Max?' Abby calls from the back of the line. I think she knows exactly what I was going to say.

'Nothing.'

WERE YOU GOING TO SAY YOU LUUURR–

'Shut up!' I call back. 'Tyson is trying to make it look like me – that's the prank. Was putting me out in the middle of the lake not enough for you, Tyson?'

'You've got to admit that was pretty funny.' Tyson chuckles.

'I don't have to admit anything!' I say and let one branch go.

WHACK! It smacks him in the face.

'Ow!'

He deserved that.

Suddenly I push through a particularly thick bit of scrub and what I see in front of me makes me stop abruptly.

'I guess we found the suitcase,' I whisper.

The others all push through the last of the bushes and stand next to me.

Duck whisper-quacks.

Before us is a small clearing. In the middle of it, Pip's suitcase is lying open, the contents thrown all around the clearing. But that's not the only thing that makes us gasp.

Layla's basketball is there on the ground. Kevin's hairbrush is stuck in a bush. But that's not what takes our breath away either.

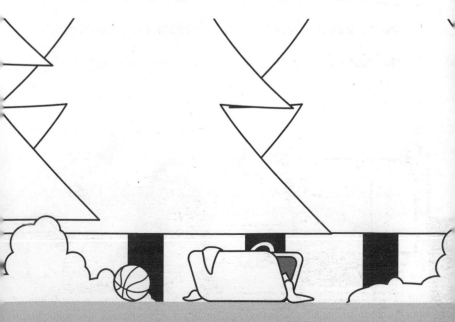

The branches around the clearing are snapped and broken. The ground is all dug up and scratched at. Little bones are scattered here and there. Only it's not even that which makes us all freeze.

It's the fact that the giant footprint Tyson found near the tent is ... Well, those footprints are everywhere.

No one speaks.

I'm having a harder and harder time convincing myself this is definitely a Tyson prank. I mean, if this is his work, he's gone to an incredible amount of effort and I can't really think why. His prank war is with me, not with Pip and Abby.

I look over at him and he seems as shocked by the scene as I am. Everyone does.

Hugo whispers, 'Is this a ... Gunker Dragon ... nest?'

Abby steps forward and faces us. Abby is nearly always serious, but this feels like a different sort of serious. She looks frightened.

No one says anything.

'No, really,' she says. 'You all know I came away on this trip feeling scared about Gunker Dragons. If you're messing with me, that's just mean. And what did I ever do to you anyway?'

Well, I have a list of things I could answer that with, but now doesn't seem to be the time.

'Seriously, Abby,' I say, 'this wasn't me.'

I turn to Tyson. He looks quite worried himself.

'I didn't do it either. I swear,' he says.

I study his face and you know what? I think I believe him.

And suddenly I feel a little chill run up and down my spine.

'As I said before, it wasn't me either,' Hugo volunteers.

It's okay, Hugo. No one ever imagined it was you.

'You're telling me the truth?' Abby asks.
'You guys didn't do this to Pip's suitcase?'

The three of us shake our heads.

Tyson and I look at each other.

THERE REALLY IS A ...

... GUNKER DRAGON.

And we're standing beside its nest. And those footprints are really big. And it must be really big. And we're not anywhere near Miss Sweet or Mr Bert. And we're going to get eaten by a monster-dinosaur. And it's going to have really big teeth. And we're going to get all crunched up in its mouth. And then we're going to be in its stomach. And we're going to be in little bits. And ...

Tyson and Hugo and I grab each other's hands and scream like a trio of terrified toddlers at a horror movie.

AAAARRRRGGGGGHHHH!!!!

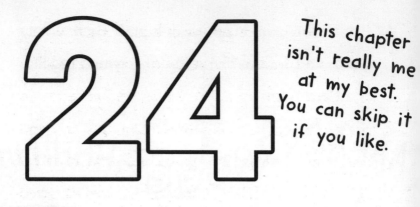

24

This chapter isn't really me at my best. You can skip it if you like.

'*Shhhhhh!*'

Abby puts one hand over my mouth and the other over Tyson's. Hugo keeps screaming. She takes her hand off Tyson's mouth and covers Hugo's. Tyson starts screaming again. She takes her hand off my mouth and keeps Hugo's and Tyson's covered. I need a break from screaming anyway.

'Will you boys shut up? It's sleeping here somewhere – we don't want to wake it!' she whisper-screams at us.

'You're right,' I say. 'Let's run and scream instead.'

I turn to flee, but Pip stands in my way.

'Can't we just get my suitcase? That's all my stuff,' she pleads with puppy-dog eyes. 'Please?'

This is my opportunity to be her hero. To bravely walk into the Gunker Dragon's nest and rescue her suitcase. Pip would tell that story for years: the day Max Walburt, the funny kid, saved her from an actual monster.

I may think Pip is pretty cool, but I'm not insane!

WAIT! JUST STAY AND KEEP WATCH FOR A MINUTE, WOULD YOU? IF YOU BOYS ARE TOO CHICKEN, THAT'S FINE, WE'LL GET THE SUITCASE OURSELVES. JUST WAIT AND TELL US IF ANYTHING'S COMING, WOULD YOU?

I'm about to run when Hugo says, 'Sure,' and Tyson says, 'Okay,' and Duck quacks.

Well, I can't be the only one who runs, can I?

And as long as the Gunker Dragon eats Hugo first, I should still be able to make it out.

'Fine,' I say, 'but be quick.'

Abby and Pip dart to the centre of the clearing and start picking up Pip's things and throwing them into the suitcase. Tyson and I look at each other.

I don't get frightened very often. Mostly just scary movies, dogs and brussels sprouts. Those tiny, stinky cabbages are freaky! But right now I'm really feeling my hair standing on end. I can see Tyson and Hugo are feeling it too.

'Where do you think it is?' I whisper to Tyson.

His eyes are wide. 'I don't know. Do you think it can see us?'

Oh, there's a thought. Is it watching us this very moment? Trying to decide who to eat first?

Hugo starts to cry. He's always been a bit of a crier, but it's completely understandable that he's turning on the waterworks now. We're about to be dragon food.

I DON'T WANT TO DIE! AND I DON'T WANT YOU TWO TO DIE EITHER! I'M SORRY ABOUT THE BEANS, TYSON!

Tyson starts to cry too. All right, this is getting a bit much.

'That's okay. I'm sorry about putting you guys out on the lake!' Tyson sobs. 'And for the snake in your sleeping bag, Max.'

Yeah, yeah. Keep going. What's that tingling feeling in my eyes?

'And for trying to make you pee on the bus,' Tyson continues.

Oh, no. I better not cry too. This is ridiculous! Then again, maybe this is what you do before you die? Maybe that's the best time to have a good cry?

I can't even stop it. It's like there's a firefighter inside my head who decides to turn on her hose and shoot water out of my eyes.

Wwwaaaaaaaahhhhhhhh!

The three of us stand there crying. If it wasn't so terrifying, it would be incredibly embarrassing. We look like three babies who have lost their dummies. I'm glad no one can see us right now.

'If we do die though,' I continue, 'it'll be really cool hanging out with you two in heaven!'

Quack.

Duck has his wings on his hips.

'You too, Duck,' I add. 'You too. Although I'm not sure ducks get to go to heaven.'

Duck scowls and waddles off in a huff to help the girls. As I watch him go, I think about how brave Abby and Pip are, and I stop sobbing for a moment. I mean, even knowing there is a monster here somewhere, they're still taking their time collecting all Pip's bits and pieces, trusting us to keep watch. There's no way I'd be doing that. Girls! I just do not understand them!

They're not really going that fast either.

And did I just hear them giggle?

I look at Tyson and Hugo. They heard it too.

The girls just giggled! At a time like this! We're all about to get eaten by a monster, and they're taking their time and having a little chuckle to themselves. What could possibly be funny?

Suddenly Hugo's eyes narrow behind his steamed-up glasses. 'Max, when did we first hear about Gunker Dragons?' he whispers.

'Oh, I don't know? When we were getting on the bus, I think. Yeah, Abby wanted to bring her dog Steve to help protect her from them. As much as I hate dogs, that might not have been such a bad idea. Why?'

'I was just thinking ...' Hugo wonders out loud.

Tyson wipes the tears from his face. 'Pip first mentioned them before that,' he says. 'It was the day before we left for camp, after I tipped water all over your head, Max. When you left, I told Pip that boys are better at pranks than girls. Then we had dinner and she spoke to Abby on the phone for ages. After that, she was telling me all about how Abby was scared of some monsters that lived out at the lake we were going to. I wasn't really paying that much attention.'

'I told Abby girls were no good at pranks too,' I say.

'Do you ever remember anyone knowing anything about Gunker Dragons, except for Abby and Pip?' Hugo asks. 'Abby told Miss Sweet about them, but she'd never heard of them. That was a bit strange.'

'And it was Pip's idea to tell scary stories around the campfire,' Tyson says. 'That's when Abby told us all about the dragons.'

'People's stuff went missing the next morning and then Pip talked about monsters when we were going canoeing,' I mumble, thinking about what this means.

'Pip apparently saw one out in the water, but Miss Sweet couldn't find it,' Hugo says.

'And when we were stuck on the lake, it was Pip and Abby who were freaking about the Gunkers,' I say, 'but it was Abby who paddled out to get us.'

'Just like it's Pip and Abby taking their time collecting Pip's things while there's supposedly a Gunker Dragon hunting us …' Tyson adds.

We all look at each other. Then we look over at the girls. They can't hear us, but they sure are taking their sweet time.

No way! I can't believe it. Really? This whole time Tyson and I have been in our prank war, there's been another enemy who's been working on the most epic prank against us? They've been working on it for days too! They've set this whole thing up and they started before we even left for camp! And they made us cry!

Tyson, Hugo and I all stare at each other.

BOYS, WE ARE STILL AT WAR.

25

I'm hitting myself in the head. I can't believe she got me with Gunker Dragons! Really, Max? You turned into a crybaby for flipping imaginary dragons?

DO YOU BELIEVE IN UNICORNS TOO?

'Don't feel bad. They got all of us,' Tyson says. 'The question is, what are we going to do about it?'

Hugo tries to explain the saying 'Your

enemy's enemy is your friend', but Tyson and I don't have time to try to understand that. It's time for us to join forces. There's no way Abby and Pip are going to make us cry and get away with it.

'The thing is, they don't know that we know what they've done,' I whisper to Tyson. 'And they think you and I hate each other, so they would never suspect we might work together to prank them back.'

'The greatest prank a prankster ever pulled was convincing the prank-ee he didn't exist,' Hugo butts in. We still have no idea what he's going on about.

'Do you want to do this?' I ask Tyson.

'You bet,' he replies and puts his fist out for a fist bump. Unfortunately I go in for the high five and just end up holding his fist. We'll probably have to work on that.

But first, we need to come up with a plan.

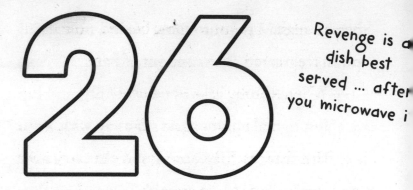

Revenge is a dish best served ... after you microwave i

Pip and Abby return with the suitcase all put back together. I can't believe I only just notice the suitcase is in really good condition, even though it's supposed to have been mauled by a Gunker Dragon. I'm still mentally kicking myself for being fooled by Abby Purcell of all people!

'Did you see any sign of the monster?' Pip asks.

Everything in me wants to just mock what she said and reveal that their plan is foiled, but no! This will work so much better if Tyson, Hugo and I play along as we agreed.

'I don't think so. Something did move over

there though.' I point to some bushes, pretending to still feel scared. 'Let's get out of here.'

'Where?' Abby asks nervously.

'Just there.' I point again. 'Do you want some help with that case? Because Tyson can carry it for you if you're not strong enough.'

Tyson frowns. 'Hey!'

Abby fumes. 'I can carry the case just fine, thank you very much! I don't need help.'

I lead the group again, although this time I take them a slightly different way. We go down one path for a bit and then I veer slightly to the right, straight for a little bit more and then slightly to the right again.

Duck quacks at me. He knows this is not the way we came and he's not in on our plan. I give him the look that says, 'It's-okay-Duck-I've-got-this-under-control-and-I'll-explain-it-all-to-you-on-the-way-home-although-that-will-be-difficult-because-you'll-have-to-hide-in-my-backpack-again-oops-sorry.'

We walk.

And we walk.

And we walk some more.

By continuing to steer us a slightly different way, I manage to get us to miss our campground altogether. Which is the plan.

'This feels a lot further than when we walked out here,' Pip says.

'We're almost there, I think,' I reply.

'It's been ages!' Tyson calls from the back. 'Where are you taking us, Max?'

'Shut up! It's not easy being the leader, especially with you whining all the time.'

'Who made you the leader anyway?' Abby asks. 'Tyson, you have a watch. What's the time? If we're not careful, Max will have us missing the bus home.'

'Um, it says it's two o'clock,' Tyson replies.

Everyone stops cold.

Tyson holds up his watch. 'That's what it says.'

Abby's eyes go wide with panic. Pip starts shaking her head frantically. Hugo looks confused.

'It can't be,' I whisper.

'The bus is supposed to leave at two o'clock!' Abby says. 'Have we really been walking for that long?'

'You did take a very long time picking up all Pip's stuff,' I throw in for good measure. Abby scowls. 'You must be getting very tired carrying that suitcase. Would you like some help?'

I SAID I'M FINE!

WHAT IF WE MISS THE BUS?

'Don't worry. Miss Sweet is not going to leave without us, I don't think,' I say. Then I pretend to look puzzled. 'Although I'm not really sure where we are ...'

Abby drops the suitcase so she has two hands to hit me with.

'It's okay, it's okay!' I protest. 'I think we're probably almost there. Let's just hurry up a bit. You're walking quite slowly, Abby. Are you sure you don't want Tyson to carry –?'

Abby looks like she wants to pull my toes off one by one.

I lead the group forward again. It should be just a little bit further ahead. 'Come on, everyone! We're almost there!'

We race through the bushes and branches until suddenly we stumble out of the trees into ... a completely empty clearing.

Everyone comes crashing in behind me.

The suitcase gets dropped.

Abby's jaw is open so wide it almost lands on the ground next to the case.

We look. There are no tents. There are no canoes. There is no bus. Our food is not there and neither are any of our bags.

EVERYONE'S GONE.

'They ... left us here?' Pip murmurs.

Abby drops to her knees in the dirt. 'I don't believe this. I *can't* believe this. This cannot be happening.'

'I really didn't think they would leave without us,' I say.

Duck is quacking angrily.

'I guess we're going to be spending another night out here ...' Tyson says.

'With no tents and no food,' I add. 'All alone.'

'And don't forget the Gunker Dragon,' Hugo says.

'What?' Abby looks up.

I pretend to be flabbergasted. 'How could you forget the whole reason we came walking out here?' I exclaim. 'The Gunker Dragon!'

Abby stands and her shoulders slump. She looks at Pip and Pip looks back. They seem to be having one of those silent conversations that girls are so good at. I can never understand how they do that.

'There ... is no Gunker Dragon,' Abby admits eventually.

'WHAT?' Tyson, Hugo and I all yell together.

WE MADE IT UP.
WE'RE REALLY SORRY.

'You made it up!' I gasp, faking disbelief.
Abby nods.

'What about the whole I've-been-reading-the-scary-history-of-Lake-Quiet stuff?' I ask.

'That's not true either,' Abby says. 'I'd never heard of Lake Quiet before this trip.'

'So are Gunker Dragons just extinct or did they never even exist?' Tyson asks.

Pip and Abby both drop their heads.

'They never even existed. We ... invented them,' Pip says.

They look *sooo* guilty.

YOU SAID GIRLS WEREN'T GOOD AT PRANKS, SO WE DECIDED TO PRANK YOU.

I slap my hand against my chest and gasp, pretending to be shocked.

'And we got you pretty good,' Abby continues. 'We dragged the suitcase into the woods and set up the dragon nest. We even scattered the leftover chicken bones from last night's dinner on the ground. It was super gross, but it felt worth it when we made you cry …'

'Now it feels pretty dumb though,' Pip adds quickly. 'Because we've missed the bus and I *really* don't want to be stuck out in the woods for the night without a tent.'

'Yeah. Great prank, guys,' Tyson says sarcastically.

'You must be feeling pretty bad right about now,' Hugo adds.

They both nod.

'We're sorry. We didn't mean for this to happen,' Abby says.

Did she really just say that? I don't believe it. Abby Purcell just apologised for something! This is the most amazing day in all of human history. To be honest, I never thought I'd live to see it! I would have paid good money for tickets to watch Abby Purcell say sorry!

I look over at Tyson and smile. He grins at Hugo. Abby and Pip notice.

'What?' Pip asks, confused.

'Why are you boys smiling? What's going on?' Abby demands.

WE JUST GOT YOU SO GOOD!

Tyson, Hugo and I burst out laughing. And then it all just comes tumbling out in mad excitement.

'What's the real time, Tyson?' I ask.

'Oh, hang on a minute,' he says. 'Let me just put my watch back to where it's supposed to be. Oh, look at that, it's only actually eleven o'clock. We've been gone for about twenty minutes. Plenty of time!'

Pip and Abby look at each other, wide eyed.

'Then where is everyone?' Pip asks, pointing to the campsite.

'This is not our campsite,' Hugo explains, grinning. 'It's one campsite over. There are identical campgrounds all the way along this lake. We just took you to the next one!'

Duck quacks, trying to tell us that's what he's been saying the whole time.

'So you knew we were faking about the Gunker Dragon?' Pip asks.

'Of course we did,' I reply. 'Turns out, Tyson and I are smarter than you think.'

'And we make a pretty good team!' he adds.

'But you two hate each other!' Abby says. Her whole body is shaking like there's a volcano beginning to erupt from her toes and it's going to blow the top of her head off.

This is the best ever!

'I think we have more in common than we thought,' I say, grinning at Tyson. 'Like being awesome.'

'And winning prank wars!' Tyson holds out his fist and we do our first successful fist bump!

Abby and Pip look at each other.

'You think this means you won the prank war?' Abby asks.

'Of course it does,' I say.

'I don't know.' Abby shrugs. 'What do you think, Pip?'

'I seem to remember you three sobbing like babies back there,' she says.

'Yeah, that's right,' Abby adds. 'I don't think winners do that.'

'No one knows about that!' Tyson exclaims.

What's going on here?

'We do,' Abby says.

WHAT ARE YOU GOING TO DO?
TELL EVERYONE WE CRIED AT YOUR STUPID
MADE-UP DRAGON? NO ONE WOULD BELIEVE THAT!

Pip pulls her phone out of her pocket and holds it up. 'They don't need to believe it,' she says.

'The whole class can watch it.' Abby grins. 'All the way home.'

Tyson, Hugo and I look at Pip's phone in terror. Sure enough, playing on the screen is a video of the three of us crying our little hearts out. While we thought they were taking a long time packing up the suitcase, they'd actually been secretly filming us!

The two girls stand next to each other with huge smiles on their faces. 'It's over, boys.'

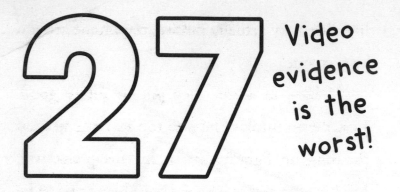

27 Video evidence is the worst!

Once we get back to our real campsite, we pack up. It turns out Miss Sweet has become so stressed by this whole camping trip thing (she's muttering to herself, 'I'm never doing this again. I'm *never* doing this again.') she didn't even notice the five of us had wandered off into the woods for half an hour. She just thinks we're slow at packing up our tents, which, of course, we are.

Pip's phone goes flying around the campsite – they don't wait until the bus ride home. I guess that will be a good opportunity for everyone to watch it for a second time. Once they've finished laughing, that is. I've never seen a video go viral like that – by actually passing the phone around to everyone!

I have to admit they got us pretty good. I can't even think of how to top it. I was so busy focusing on fighting Tyson in this prank war, I didn't even realise we were both being played by the girls this whole time. Turns out they're not so bad at pranks after all.

Finally it's time to get back on the bus. We load our things into the cargo hold with a little help from Mr Bert. Luckily this time I

don't need to put Duck in my backpack, which he seems quite relieved about. Miss Sweet has just given up and says he can sit in a box by the window. I've never seen Duck so happy.

'Hey, Tyson – come sit here!' I call out. He drops into the seat next to me and Hugo hops in behind us.

'Hugo,' Pip says. 'Do you mind if I sit next to you?'

Abby plops down next to Layla across the aisle and I suddenly realise we're all sitting in exactly the same seats we were in on our way to camp, only now we all seem a little happier about it.

This fresh air stuff is pretty powerful!

'I want to talk about my book,' Hugo announces. Oh, not this again! I forgot all about his book. 'I've made a decision –'

'Me too!' I interrupt. 'I don't want you to write a book about me any more!'

Before Mr Bert starts the bus, Miss Sweet stands up and gives us all a lecture about pranks, because I guess that's what they taught her to do at teacher school. She looks like she just wants to go home and sleep for three weeks.

She also has to give us all a punishment for mucking up so much. I can tell she doesn't really have the energy for that either, but I think there's a line about consequences in her job description.

'Given we have spent so much time talking about animals that may or may not be extinct, or even exist at all, I've decided that next week we are going to start raising money for endangered animals. You will each choose an animal and a charity that supports your animal, you will tell us all about your chosen charity and then you're all going to work your little bottoms off trying to raise as much money for your charity as you can. You may have spent the past three days fighting each other in a prank war, but it's going to be peacetime in Redhill now. You can compete with each other to see who is better at doing something positive for the world.'

Ooh. What animal am I going to choose? That could be something for Tyson and me to discuss on the way home. Who would have thought?

You know what else is strange? Ever since Tyson and I worked out that being funny kids together is better than being a funny kid on your own, I've kind of lost interest in trying to talk to Pip all the time. It's like there was this switch

that's just been turned off. That will make things a lot easier.

Besides, planning and scheming with Tyson is much more fun!

It's a great relief really, because I was a little nervous when we started this book that it was going to turn into a love story. *So gross!* But you'll be relieved to see it's okay! It didn't become a love story at all!

Then I hear Pip say behind me:

HUGO, HAS ANYONE EVER TOLD YOU THAT YOU HAVE VERY MUSCLY ARMS?

Okaaaaaaayyyyy. Maybe I spoke too soon …

THE END

What did you think?

Kids all over the world
are emailing Matt
their Funny Kid reviews!

Email him yours!

matt.stanton@gmail.com

Have you read the very first
Funny Kid book?
FUNNY KID FOR PRESIDENT!

This one is BLUE
and someone poops in
the storeroom!

And don't forget
Funny Kid #2!
FUNNY KID STAND UP!

This one is RED
and I get heckled
by a clown!

Are you ready for Funny Kid #4?
Look out for

FUNNY KID GET LICKED!

It's ORANGE, you know,
like an ... orange.

Matt Stanton is a bestselling children's author and illustrator, with half a million books in print. He is the co-creator of the mega-hits *There Is a Monster Under My Bed Who Farts* and *This Is a Ball*. *Funny Kid for President* debuted as the #1 Australian kids' book and is fast winning legions of fans around the world.

mattstanton.net

Come and subscribe to
Matt's YouTube Channel!

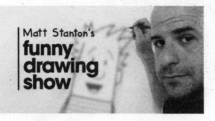

We learn to draw funny stuff!

Talk about how to write funny stories!

And sometimes we launch a book out of a cannon!

MattStantonTV
youtube.com/mattstanton